DOG
TALES

EMILY RODDA

DOG TALES

Illustrated by Janine Dawson

An Omnibus Book from Scholastic Australia

LEXILE™ 720

Omnibus Books
175–177 Young Street, Parkside SA 5063
an imprint of Scholastic Australia Pty Ltd (ABN 11 000 614 577)
PO Box 579, Gosford NSW 2250.
www.scholastic.com.au

Part of the Scholastic Group
Sydney · Auckland · New York · Toronto · London · Mexico City ·
New Delhi · Hong Kong · Buenos Aires · Puerto Rico

First published in 2001.
Reprinted in 2002, 2003, 2010 (three times), 2011.
First published in this edition in 2013.
Text copyright © Emily Rodda, 2001.
Illustrations copyright © Janine Dawson, 2001.

National Library of Australia Cataloguing-in-Publication entry
Rodda, Emily.
Dog tales.
ISBN 978 1 74299 016 3.
1. Dogs – Juvenile fiction. I. Dawson, Janine. II. Title.
A823.3

Typeset in 12/18 pt Berkeley by Clinton Ellicott, Adelaide.
Printed and bound by McPherson's Printing Group, Victoria.
Scholastic Australia's policy, in association with McPherson's Printing
Group, is to use papers that are renewable and made efficiently from
wood grown in sustainable forests, so as to minimise its
environmental impact.

10 9 8 7 6 5 4 3 2 1   13 14 15 / 0

Dog Tales is dedicated to those special dogs Minnie, Master, Bo, Cherry, Gina, Poppy, Mattie, Deakin, Barney, Sam, Max 1 and Max 2 and Sunny, without whose inspiration it could never have been written. And, also, of course, to Rita, Ruby, Rose, Dizzy, Oscar and Tenzin, goats of renown.

CONTENTS

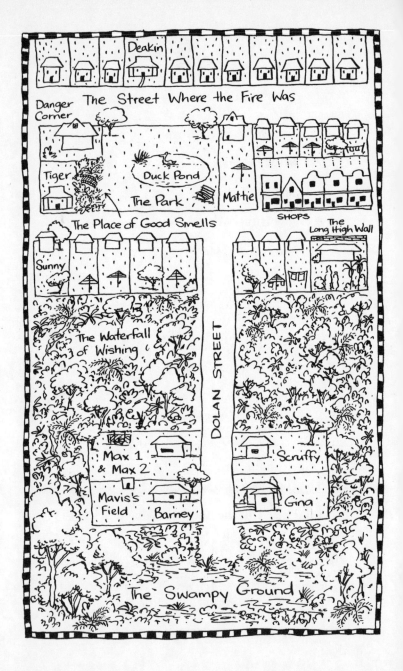

1 The Dolan Street Dogs

The Dolan Street dogs were Max 1, Max 2, Barney, Scruffy, Gina and Mavis. Mavis was actually a goat, but she did not know this, and none of the others liked to tell her.

'Though you'd think she'd realise,' Barney often said, in the special low voice he used for delicate matters. 'After all, Mavis lives in a field. And she eats green stuff, which everyone knows is only good for curing bellyache.'

Whenever Barney said that, Scruffy, who was a small, raggedy white dog, always kept very quiet. She quite enjoyed a piece of apple, a few grapes or a piece of cabbage herself. And, of course, she and

1

Mavis had exactly the same colouring.

Scruffy thought that it was quite possible that she, too, was a goat. She was very much shorter than Mavis. But then, she was still young.

The idea of her possible goatness made Scruffy feel quite excited and important, but also a bit scared. She found Mavis very impressive, and would not at all have minded being so big. On the other hand, she did not like the thought of sleeping in Mavis's draughty shed in the field behind Barney's house. She much preferred her own home.

She said nothing to any of the other dogs, but every day she examined her reflection in the long mirror at the end of her hallway, to check her head for horns.

The Dolan Street dogs had been neighbours for a long time. Scruffy was the youngest of the group. She lived next door to Gina, a kind and gentle golden-haired Labrador who was her best friend.

Across the road lived Max 1 and Max 2, the twins.

They were young and full of energy. Their smooth fur was various shades of brown. They had floppy ears, short legs and stubby tails, and looked very like one another, though not like any other dog Scruffy had ever seen.

Gina, who was very interested in family history, said she believed the Maxes had more than a little Beagle in their ancestry. Also Dachshund, she said. And possibly Spaniel. With a touch of Terrier, for snappiness. And a few other things.

Gina said that Scruffy was probably a sort of Terrier too, because she liked to dig holes. But, Gina always added hastily, no one could accuse Scruffy of snappiness. In fact, she said, no one could be less snappy than Scruffy, who was as kind and considerate as any Labrador, despite her long hair, and the shortness of her legs and tail.

She never seemed to consider the possibility that Scruffy might be a goat.

Perhaps, Scruffy thought, it's because I'm still so small, and Gina doesn't know what young goats look like. Also, maybe she doesn't think of it because Mavis doesn't dig. But if I *am* a goat, I suppose I'll just grow out of digging. She made a firm resolution to remember where both her bones were, and dig them up, before that time came.

Barney lived next door to the Maxes. Or, as he always said, the Maxes lived next door to *him*. No one knew exactly how old Barney was. It was certain, however, that he was by far the oldest resident in Dolan Street, just as his house was the oldest house.

Barney had rough blue-grey fur with a few black spots. His muzzle was quite white. Scruffy knew that Barney was very wise, because Barney often said so, and he was always right.

Barney had brought Mavis up. He had taught her everything she knew, just as *his* guardian, a grand old dog called Buster, had taught him.

Barney couldn't remember exactly why he had forgotten to tell Mavis she was a goat. He said he must have had a lot on his mind at the time.

✄✄✄

The dogs' homes were the only houses in Dolan Street, which was a short, narrow road that led down a steep hill.

The top part of the road was lined on both sides with thick trees and bushes, the homes of various creatures who preferred to live in the open air. The four houses were all at the bottom of the hill, where the road ended in a swampy, overgrown patch of land owned by a large and noisy group of frogs.

When Max 1 and Max 2 were bored, which was

often, or when they wanted to annoy Barney, which was even more often, they said that they wished they lived in one of the houses near the park at the top of the hill. Around those houses there were traffic lights, street lights and shops. Also lots of food, just lying on the ground for anyone to find, especially beside certain garbage bins.

Barney said that the Maxes didn't know how lucky they were. He said that *he* couldn't imagine anything worse than being crowded in with a lot of other dogs, and plagued by traffic noise. When the Maxes were as old and wise as *he* was, he said, they'd learn that Dolan Street was the best street on earth.

Mavis said she wouldn't know. She'd never *been* anywhere else. But if traffic was noisier than the Dolan Street birds chattering and gossiping all day and the Dolan Street frogs having wild parties every night, she was pleased to be away from it.

The birds annoyed Mavis particularly because, as well as being noisy and extremely silly, they liked to perch on her head, especially when she was having a doze. She said their feet tickled, and they often carelessly left feathers, and even the remains of their snacks, in her hair.

Once, in fact, a small and more than usually silly bird had left something worse, but that was never

spoken of in company. The bird was too embarrassed by its mistake to say anything to its family or friends, and Barney, who was the only dog other than Mavis to know about the unpleasantness, had agreed with her that it was best to keep the matter quiet. There was a strong chance that Max 1 and Max 2 might make rude jokes about it, if ever they found out. They were not known for their good manners.

༄༅༄༅

The Dolan Street dogs were not the only dogs in their neighbourhood, of course. Spending their days quietly at the bottom of their hill as they did, however, they did not mix with others very often.

Scruffy, who was rather shy, did not mind this at all. The Dolan Street group was more than enough for her. Besides, when she, Max 1, Max 2 and Gina were taking their Pets for walks in the evenings, they all had a chance to meet other dogs, or exchange a few words with them as they passed their houses.

Even Gina had to admit that a few of these dogs were not very pleasant. No one liked the two Rottweilers at Danger Corner, for example. They were most unfriendly. Gina said they'd probably had unhappy puppyhoods.

Then there was the mystery dog behind The Long High Wall. He shouted insults at anyone who passed. The gossip was that his nickname was Garbage Guts, and he had been a champion jumper and master escaper at his previous home.

Gina thought that living behind a wall that was too high even for him to jump must have made Garbage Guts very bitter, though this was no excuse for being rude.

Other meetings were usually pleasant, though quite formal. The Dolan Street dogs did not know some of their far neighbours at all, and many they knew just to sniff to.

They did, however, have four special friends. Sunny, the glossy black-and-brown dog who lived beside The Waterfall of Wishing, was one of these. Mattie, the Poodle near the park at the top of the hill, was another. And then there was Tiger, the

Scotch Terrier next door to The Place of Good Smells, and Deakin, the Boxer on The Street Where the Fire Was.

All of them were interesting to meet, always full of news and gossip, though Max 1 and Max 2 would have got on with Tiger rather better if they had followed Gina's advice and not teased him about the red checked coat he wore in the winter.

Barney and Mavis never went for walks. They preferred to stay home and sleep, and their Pets, Bert and Alice, agreed with them. All the same, Barney and Mavis knew most of the neighbourhood dogs quite well, by sound if not by sight.

Barney always answered politely if he heard dogs calling out at night, and of course occasionally one or two of them would walk down Dolan Street, with their Pets or alone. When they reached his house, Barney would always shout to them over the fence, reminding them who he was.

These days, he mostly shouted without bothering to move from his usual spot on the grass. But Mavis said that in the old days, when he was more energetic, Barney would run up and down the fence, and even jump up on the gate, rattling it and trying to push it open.

Once, when he was doing this, the gate actually

did open. Unfortunately, that was the day that the passing dogs were the Danger Corner Rottweilers.

The result, for Barney, was embarrassing, and he hadn't jumped up on the gate since. In fact, before lying down in the sun these days, he always checked the lock.

❧❧❧

Every morning, after their Pets had gone out in their cars, the Dolan Street dogs met in Barney's front yard.

The Maxes came under the fence that divided their property from Barney's. Gina and Scruffy came through a gap in the wire on the other side, after threading their way through the swampy ground where the frogs lived.

First they listened to the morning news echoing down the hill, and joined in if they had anything of interest to add. Then they chatted to one another until it was time to go inside to watch 'Dog Hospital', which was by far their favourite TV show.

If the Pets thought about it at all (which Barney said he doubted), they believed that nothing much happened in Dolan Street while they were away. But, as even Max 1 and Max 2 admitted, when they weren't teasing Barney, life in the street wasn't nearly as quiet and ordinary as it seemed.

Many quite interesting, unusual things happened

at the bottom of the Dolan Street hill. The dogs, of course, were always at the centre of them, for, after all, they were almost always the only ones at home when the unusual things occurred.

The Dolan Street dogs thought this was just as well. Pets were very sensitive. They became worried and over-excited very easily.

What would they have said if they had known about The Haunting, for example? Or about The Blackmail? Or The Night the Burglars Came? Or even Barney's Magic …?

2 Barney's Magic

One morning, the dogs were lying in Barney's front yard, enjoying the peace that always fell on their street after the Pets had left in their cars for the day.

Mavis had found a sock on the grass and was chewing it with her usual thoughtful delicacy. She was the only one with anything to eat.

'The trouble with mornings,' Max 1 complained, after a while, 'is that they're so far away from dinnertime.'

Scruffy agreed. She would have liked to dig up her second-best bone, but the more she thought about it, the more she couldn't remember where she'd buried it.

'I'd kill for a dog biscuit,' growled Max 2. 'But the packet's empty.'

He snapped irritably at a fly, and caught it by mistake. A passing bird shrieked and flew off in great excitement to tell its friends that the Dolan Street dogs had started eating insects.

'That's not true!' Gina shouted. 'He didn't eat it! Look! He's spitting it out!'

The bird took no notice. It reached the trees in the swampy ground, and a great twittering and chattering began.

Barney glared at Max 2. 'Now see what you've done,' he growled. 'Next thing, they'll be flying off and telling the whole neighbourhood a pack of lies about us.'

'What do I care?' Max 2 mumbled. 'I'll be dead of hunger by tonight, anyway.'

Barney shook his head sadly. He always kept a few tasty morsels in a safe place, but he never ate these till the afternoon. And it was quite understood that they were not for sharing.

'As Old Buster always used to tell me,' he said,

'self-control is a dog's best friend. Wise is the dog who saves, for the days of foolish dogs are long and hungry.'

Max 1 and Max 2 groaned. Self-control was not their strong point.

'Want a worm for dessert?' screeched a bird, zooming overhead.

The dogs pretended to ignore it. When birds got really silly, that was the only thing to do.

'I *must* tell you what Caroline did last night,' Gina began. 'It was so *cute*. She …'

Max 1 and Max 2 groaned softly and started to practise balancing leaves on their noses. Barney and Mavis closed their eyes. Scruffy suspected that they were not very interested in Gina's stories about her Pet.

Caroline was very intelligent, with beautiful, expressive eyes. She was an excellent protector, Gina said, and a wonderful companion as well. More like a dog than a Pet. It was clear to everyone that Gina believed Caroline was by far the most adorable Pet in Dolan Street.

Even Scruffy sometimes found Gina's Caroline stories a tiny bit boring, if they were very long. But she always listened anyway, laughing in all the right places. She didn't want to hurt Gina's feelings.

Today, Gina's story was about how Caroline had brought home two little iced cakes, and had pretended for quite a long time that she was going to eat both of them herself. That had been a very good joke, and Gina laughed a lot while she was telling the story, but all this talk of cakes just made everyone even hungrier.

The story had just finished when a lost truck came rumbling down Dolan Street. It rattled past Barney's fence, reached the end of the road, then turned and struggled off again.

Barney got up slowly, shook himself once, twice, three times, and went around to the side of his house to check his food bowl.

Max 1 and Max 2 sniggered and nudged one another, but Mavis, Scruffy and Gina watched carefully.

Once, they knew, Barney had experienced something wonderful after a truck came down Dolan Street, turned and went away again. All the dogs had heard the story a hundred times, for Barney never got tired of telling it.

It was years ago, in autumn. A crisp, bright day, full of smells and promise.

Barney had enjoyed his breakfast of biscuit and tea, as usual. His food bowl was clean when he left it.

Spotless, Barney said. He had come to sit in the sun at the front of his house, as usual. The Pets had left in their cars, as usual. Then, after a while, the truck had come.

As it happened, Barney was particularly thirsty that morning. After the truck turned and left, he got up. There were autumn leaves on the grass. He had to shake himself three times before his rough grey fur was clean. Then he plodded around to the side of his house to get a drink.

And there, in his food bowl, was a whole sausage.

Scruffy could imagine the scene. The food bowl, silver and gleaming. The sausage, huge and perfect, lying there inside it. Barney, staring, hardly able to believe his eyes.

As Barney put it, at that moment time seemed to

stand still. He sniffed the sausage. He licked it. Then he knew.

This was Magic. Somehow, he had stumbled upon a Sausage Appearing Spell.

Thinking about it afterwards, long and hard, Barney remembered the truck. And he remembered that after it had turned and left he had shaken himself three times before going to the side of the house. He realised that somehow these two things must be linked.

For the sausage had been there. It had appeared out of thin air.

Magic.

Ever since, Barney had been trying to repeat the Spell that had made the sausage appear in his food bowl. Every time a truck came down Dolan Street, turned and went back up again, he tried to do exactly what he had done on that long ago, fateful day.

So far, he hadn't succeeded in making another sausage appear. He'd tried shaking fast. Shaking slowly. Shaking with his head up. Shaking with his head down. But nothing worked.

'Try it with one foot in the air,' Max 1 smirked. And Barney did.

'Try it with two feet in the air,' Max 2 tittered. And

Barney did that, too. But when the twins suggested he try three feet in the air, he just sniffed. He was too old a dog to fall for tricks like that.

'One day,' he said to Max 1 and Max 2 severely, 'I will re-discover the Sausage Appearing Spell. Then I will have a sausage every day for the rest of my life. And you two will laugh on the other side of your faces!'

The Maxes didn't believe it. They thought that Barney's Pets, Bert and Alice, had put the sausage in the food bowl just before they left in their car that morning.

But Barney shook his head and pointed out that his Pets had never done such a thing before, so why would they have started on *that* particular morning?

And why would they have given him a perfectly good sausage, when they enjoyed eating sausages themselves? The sausage in his bowl was a perfect specimen. Nicely aged, and black at both ends.

'Pets are like that,' said Max 1. 'Who knows what goes on in their minds?'

But Scruffy, Gina and Mavis believed that Barney was right. He was far older and wiser than Max 1 and Max 2. And, after all, it couldn't have been just a coincidence that the sausage had appeared right on the very day that the truck came and Barney shook three times, could it?

⤞⤝ ⤞⤝ ⤞⤝

'Oh, I really think this time he's done it! I feel it in my bones!' breathed Gina, crossing her paws as Barney disappeared around the side of the house.

'Want to bet?' jeered Max 1.

The birds were chattering in low voices, watching Barney with interest.

'Silly things!' said Mavis in disgust. 'And that reminds me. What about my tree?'

For months Mavis had been talking about planting a tree beside her shed in the field. She wanted it for summer shade, and to make her home more attractive. She hoped, also, that if the birds had somewhere else to rest when they visited the field, they would leave her head alone. The trouble was, she couldn't decide what kind of tree to plant. She only knew that it must be one that was bare in winter. Her shed, she said, needed full sun in cold weather.

Unfortunately, almost all the trees in Dolan Street kept their leaves all year round, and none of the ones that didn't appealed to Mavis. The Maxes said she was being too choosy, but she said she couldn't plant just *any* old tree. There was only going to be one, so it had to be special.

Scruffy was keen to help. After all, one day she might be living in the field herself. She agreed with Mavis that a nice shady tree would improve things greatly.

Every now and then, when she came back from a walk, she brought Mavis a leafy twig from a different tree. Then she tried to describe the tree from which it had come. Each time she hoped that Mavis would decide that *this* tree was the perfect one.

But Mavis was very hard to please.

She never failed to thank Scruffy very politely, and to examine the new twig carefully. In the end, though, she always shook her head and said that she was sorry, but this particular tree didn't seem quite right.

It sounded too big or too small, she would say. Or its bark was too rough or too smooth. Or its leaves were too limp or too prickly, too green or not green enough.

'You'll never decide, Mavis,' Max 1 and Max 2 would say, then. 'At this rate, you'll never get a tree!'

Mavis would toss her head and turn away.

'Muzzle your traps, you two!' Barney would growl. 'If Mavis wants a tree, she'll have one.'

Then he'd add, under his breath: 'Mind you, there was never a tree in the field in Old Buster's day. And what was good enough for him is good enough for me.'

And Gina would shake her head at the Maxes and say, 'It's a very important decision. Mavis has a right to take her time.'

Lately, though, even Gina seemed to be losing patience. In fact, she'd privately suggested to Scruffy that perhaps Scruffy shouldn't bother bringing leafy twigs home any more, because it was a waste of time.

It *was* disappointing, but as Mavis always enjoyed eating the twigs afterwards, Scruffy didn't feel that her efforts were totally wasted. And she still wanted to help.

'I've been thinking – there are a lot of baby oak trees under the big old oak in The Place of Good Smells, Mavis,' she said now. 'I could easily dig one up, and bring it home for you.'

Gina tore her eyes away from the side of the house and nodded. 'Perfect!' she agreed enthusiastically. 'Oak trees make wonderful shade.'

Mavis sniffed. 'Sorry, but I don't think I like oak trees,' she said in a muffled voice. She had reached the heel of the sock, and it was rather tough.

'You've never even *seen* an oak tree, Mavis!' exploded Max 1.

'I have seen a *twig* from an oak tree, thank you very much,' said Mavis haughtily. 'Oak tree leaves are too frilly. And they rustle too much. Like birds' wings. They don't taste bad, I admit. But I do *not* want an oak tree beside my shed, and that's that!'

The Maxes looked at one another knowingly, but at that moment Barney came plodding back from the side of the house, and the whole tree discussion was forgotten.

'Any luck?' called Gina.

Scruffy held her breath.

Barney shook his head in frustration.

'There's still something wrong,' he said heavily. 'The truck must have been the wrong sort. Or I didn't shake myself well enough, or something. And, do you know, there was a frog in my water bowl! It's like its cheek!'

Max 2 snorted, but quietly. He couldn't afford to offend Barney just then. 'Dog Hospital' would be starting any minute, and he didn't want to miss it.

3 The Dead Dog

The dogs all trooped into Barney's living room and settled into their usual places. Then Barney turned on the TV set, and they got ready to watch the show.

There was the usual squabble because Barney would not let Max 1 and Max 2 have the remote control. Max 1 and Max 2 liked to switch channels when the ads were on. Barney liked to stay with one channel. He said that channel surfing made his head go round and round, and, anyway, he liked the ads.

Besides, the only time Max 1 and Max 2 had ever used Barney's remote control they had punched the buttons too roughly, and one had got stuck. Then, instead of seeing the last half of 'Dog Hospital' – a particularly exciting episode about a beautiful young Red Setter who had been bitten by a snake – they had to watch a program for Petlings about road safety.

By the time Barney fixed the remote control, 'Dog Hospital' had finished, so they never did find out if the Red Setter lived or died. It was very disappointing.

This day Barney kept the remote control to himself, and the friends saw 'Dog Hospital' right through.

It was the story of a Pug with worms.

Gina was very interested in it. She said it was one of the most touching things she had ever seen, and educational as well.

Scruffy didn't enjoy it very much. She found it a bit boring, and the closeups of worms made her feel queasy.

Max 1 and Max 2 kept making rude jokes about the Pug, and sniggering into the cushions. Barney, who was still rather upset about the failure of the Sausage Appearing Spell, accused them of smearing the cushions with dribble, and threatened to ban them from the house.

Mavis went to sleep.

ᢒᢃᢒᢃᢒᢃ

When 'Dog Hospital' was over, they woke Mavis and went outside again. To their great surprise, there was a perfect stranger lying on the grass.

Barney bellowed a warning, and bounded up to him, but the stranger didn't move. He just lay where he was, his eyes closed, like a bundle of wiry golden-brown fur.

Max 1 darted forward and nipped his tail, then darted quickly away again, but the stranger made no movement.

Now that they were closer, they could hear that his stomach was making horrible gurgling sounds. All that came from his lips was a low groan.

'He's sick!' Gina exclaimed in horror. 'Barney, call an ambulance!'

'The phone doesn't work,' said Mavis. 'Alice and Bert didn't pay the bill.'

'That's because you *ate* the bill, Mavis,' growled Barney. 'Admit it!'

Mavis looked at him haughtily.

'I admit nothing,' she said. 'But I would like to point out that even if we *could* ring, we could not make the Pets at the other end of the line understand us.'

'That's true,' Gina sighed. 'The poor things only understand a few words of Dog, as you know. And even then they need actions as well. An address would be quite beyond them.'

The stranger groaned again. He seemed to be trying to speak. All the dogs bent lower, so they could hear him.

'*Stomach*,' he whispered. 'Oh, the agony! Oh, the pain! I shouldn't have eaten … shouldn't have …'

His voice trailed off.

'Poison!' Gina hissed.

Wildly excited, Max 1 and Max 2 ran to the front gate and began spreading the word that there had been a poisoning in Dolan Street and help was needed urgently.

Tiger, Deakin, Sunny, Mattie and a few other dogs answered. Their voices echoed over the hill and down Dolan Street.

'Sorry! No Pets home!' 'No cars!' 'So you *were* eating insects! We didn't believe it!' 'Who ate what? Who's dead?'

'Tell them *no one* was eating insects!' roared Barney.

'Don't worry about that!' Gina exclaimed, running towards the house. 'Help him!'

Barney shook his head. 'There was none of this poisoning business when I was a pup,' he grumbled. 'Or if there was, I never heard about it. Dogs kept it to themselves. What's the world coming to when a respectable dog can't watch a bit of TV in his own house without troops of poisoned strangers barging into his yard?'

'How did he get in?' Scruffy asked. 'The gate's

locked. And he couldn't have found his way through the frogs' ground. Not without us to help.'

But the others weren't listening.

Max 1 and Max 2 were busy inviting everyone within earshot to the funeral.

Gina, her years of watching 'Dog Hospital' coming to the fore, had come back from the house with Barney's blanket, and was trying to cover the stranger with it.

Barney was objecting strongly to this. He said he wasn't going to have his blanket wrapped round a dead dog.

'He's not dead!' Gina cried.

'He soon will be,' said Barney. 'If he's eaten poison, he's a goner, and that's all there is to it. We'll have to bury him. Scruffy, start digging!'

Gina drew herself up dramatically.

'While there's life, there's hope!' she said. 'Mavis! Collect some grass to settle his stomach. Meanwhile, I'll try to make him throw up.'

'Not on my blanket, you won't!' snapped Barney. He grabbed the blanket and began trying to pull it away, but Gina held it fast.

'Scruffy, get water!' she ordered through clenched teeth.

'Scruffy, dig!' Barney growled at the same moment.

Scruffy looked desperately this way and that. She couldn't be in two places at once.

'If you take my advice, you'll dig the grave,' Mavis muttered in her ear. 'Barney's in charge of the TV, and he can hold a grudge for months. Don't I know it! I'm never going to hear the end of that phone bill. Besides, if you dig deep enough, you'll probably find underground water. Then you'll please both of them.'

Scruffy began to dig furiously, hoping against hope that Mavis was right.

'Has he snuffed it yet?' shouted Max 1, rushing back from the gate with Max 2 hard on his heels.

'Any minute now, I'd say,' said Barney. He was carefully rolling up the blanket, which he'd finally managed to snatch away from Gina.

Max 1 looked critically at the hole Scruffy was digging.

'That grave's much too small,' he said. 'It's getting nice and deep, but it's no wider than you are, Scruffy.

At this rate, we'll have to put him into it head first. And how will that look? What will our visitors think?'

'I don't give a piece of gristle for what they think!' snorted Barney, as he began to drag the blanket away to safety. 'A dead dog on my grass! What have I done to deserve this? Why oh why did he ever come in here?'

'*How* did he come in here?' asked Scruffy, from the bottom of the hole. But she might as well have been talking to herself.

Max 1 and Max 2 were arguing about which flowers to pick for the funeral. Gina was trying to push her paw down the stranger's throat to make him throw up. Barney was disappearing around the side of the house with his blanket.

Mavis had forgotten all about collecting grass, and was eating it instead.

The stranger began to choke and heave, trying to spit out Gina's paw.

'That's the way,' she said, in her best nurse-like voice. 'That's the –'

She screamed and jumped back. The stranger had opened his eyes and bitten her paw, hard.

At the same moment, there was a roar from the side of the house.

'*Who did this?*' bellowed Barney.

The stranger scrambled to his feet.

'I'm off,' he said.

As Gina, Mavis, Max 1 and Max 2 stared, he wobbled to the fence. He gathered himself up and sprang over it.

'Losers!' he said rudely, poking out his tongue. Then he began staggering up the road.

For a dying dog, he moved surprisingly quickly. By the time Barney came charging back onto the grass, he had disappeared.

'*Who tipped over the garbage bin?*' Barney snarled, fixing his friends with a furious eye. '*Who* ate all the garbage? And, more important, *who* ate the toast crust, the chicken skin and the frankfurt end *with sauce*, hidden under my bowl?'

'Not me,' mumbled Mavis quickly, through a mouthful of grass.

'Not me,' said Gina, sucking her paw.

'Not me!' panted Scruffy, from the bottom of the hole.

'Not us,' said Max 1 and Max 2 in chorus.

Barney's eyes narrowed. Then he noticed that the stranger had gone.

'Where's the dead dog?' he demanded.

'I saved him,' said Gina. 'But he was quite ungrateful.'

'And *very* inconsiderate!' fumed Max 1. 'We've got twelve dogs coming to his funeral in half an hour. What are we supposed to say to them? He never even told us his name!'

Scruffy poked her head out of the hole. She still hadn't found water, but, thank goodness, that didn't matter now.

'I think I recognised his voice,' she said brightly. 'Wasn't that Garbage Guts, the great escaper, who lives behind The Long High Wall?'

The others considered this in silence.

'You're right,' said Max 2 finally. 'He must have found a way out of his house at last.'

'He probably tunnelled,' said Max 1, nodding wisely.

'Well!' snapped Mavis, tossing her head. 'If I'd known it was Garbage Guts, I wouldn't have done a thing to help him. The remarks he calls out at night are disgraceful!'

She hadn't done a thing to help, in fact, but no one felt like saying so.

Scruffy's eyes were wide.

'He must have jumped over your front fence while we were watching TV, Barney,' she said.

'Poisoned, dying dogs can't jump over fences!' exclaimed Gina.

'Have you considered that perhaps he was perfectly all right when he came in?' asked Mavis coldly. 'And have you considered that perhaps he wasn't poisoned at all, but just had – a bellyache?'

There was another short silence while everyone thought about the garbage, and about Barney's toast crust, chicken skin and frankfurt end with sauce.

After that, there didn't seem to be very much to say.

Max 1 and Max 2 went to the gate and called out to everyone, cancelling the funeral.

Gina and Scruffy filled in the grave.

Mavis and Barney cleaned up the remains of the garbage.

Then they all went to sleep. It seemed the only sensible thing to do, under the circumstances.

4 Saving the World

The day the Dolan Street dogs saved the world began in a very ordinary way.

It was cool and the sky was heavy. It looked very much as though it was going to rain.

The birds were cross about this, and were mumbling to one another in the trees. The frogs in the swampy ground were getting excited, hoping for a real downpour.

After the Pets had left in their cars, the dogs met in Barney's yard as usual. They listened to the morning news, and were most annoyed at one particular item.

An unknown reporter claimed that Garbage Guts, the famous trickster and escaper, had helped himself to food from Dolan Street without one of the dogs there lifting a paw to stop him.

It was no wonder, the unknown reporter went on nastily, that the Dolan Street dogs were reduced to eating insects, if this was the way they protected their homes.

'I think that's Garbage Guts himself talking,' said Gina, quite fluffed up with anger.

Barney, of course, immediately tried to correct the story. But the first version, starring Garbage Guts the daring robber hero, was so much more interesting than the true one that only a few dogs took any notice.

'That miserable, thieving hound will answer to me for this!' Barney snarled. 'How dare he?'

'How dare he?' Mavis repeated, pawing the ground.

'I wish he was here now,' said Max 2, showing his teeth. 'I'd show him!'

'So would I!' growled his brother.

Scruffy was a peaceful dog generally, but on this occasion she felt quite savage.

And even Gina, whose paw was still very tender, didn't feel like calming anyone down.

Rain began falling as they went inside. It cooled none of their tempers.

'Dog Hospital' that day was about a disturbed Cocker Spaniel called Polly, who kept biting her Pets' feet.

By the end, Polly had stopped biting her Pets, but had started biting her own feet instead. Scruffy didn't think that was a very good ending at all, and Gina agreed with her.

Barney said that Polly just needed a bit of old-fashioned discipline, as far as he could see, and that Old Buster would soon have brought her into line.

The Maxes enjoyed the biting scenes, but in general thought the episode was too serious and slow. The most exciting moment for them was when Barney found a small piece of cheese in the couch.

Mavis went to sleep again.

By the time the show ended, it had begun to rain quite heavily, so they woke Mavis and had a game of carpet bowls.

It was as the game was reaching an exciting climax, with Barney leading and Mavis just a few points behind him, that the house trembled slightly, the windows rattled, and a brilliant flash lit the room.

All the dogs stiffened, and flattened their ears. Gina whimpered. Then Barney cleared his throat.

'Thunderstorm,' he said solemnly. 'Ah, I knew I shouldn't have eaten that cheese. As Old Buster, rest his bones, used to say: Cheese in the morning, wet dog's warning. Did I ever tell you about the time I –'

'No!' Max 1 yelped. His voice was high and shrill. His hair was standing on end. He was staring through the window that looked out over Mavis's field.

All the dogs ran to look.

Rain poured from the clouded sky, pounding onto a large round silver thing that had landed in the middle of the field. Lights flashed around the silver thing's rim. Despite the rain, the grass around it was scorched as if by fire.

The thing wasn't a car. It wasn't a plane. It was quite the wrong shape for either of those things – even Scruffy knew that.

The lights on the silver thing faded and went out.

A door opened at the top. The dogs saw movement. Something was coming out!

'Strangers!' yelled Barney, and bounded for the door.

'In my field!' exclaimed Mavis, and galloped after him.

The others followed more slowly. Barney and Mavis had to rush to defend their property, of course. But it seemed sensible for other dogs, who, after all, were only visitors, to be more cautious.

At the door Max 2 said he thought he felt one of his dizzy spells coming on, and perhaps they should go on without him. But after Max 1 nipped him on the tail he seemed to feel a lot better. So much better, in fact, that he led the way outside.

꼭꼭꼭

The dogs found Mavis and Barney facing a small blue-coloured Creature that stood importantly on its hind legs beside the large round silver thing. The Creature had huge blank eyes, a small mouth and no hair at all. It was wearing a thin silver suit, and was about the size of a young Pet.

But this was no Petling. Its scent was quite different – a mixture of petrol, flea soap and lizard, Scruffy thought. Not very attractive.

'What is it?' she murmured.

'It's a Creature From Outer Space!' hissed Max 1 out of the side of his mouth. 'Don't you know anything?'

Scruffy's blood ran cold. On TV, Creatures From Outer Space sometimes had laser guns. Sometimes, too, they ate Pets – and even dogs.

The frogs in the swampy ground were having a rain party. They didn't seem to care that Dolan Street was being invaded.

The birds were no help, either. They were all hiding in the trees, trying to keep dry.

The dogs were on their own.

Barney stepped forward.

'Go away,' he said fiercely, raising his voice to be heard above the frogs' singing. 'There is no parking here!'

The Creature looked at him, wiped rain from its

huge eyes, and began pushing buttons on a gadget hanging from its belt. The gadget looked like a TV remote control. As the Creature pushed at its buttons, it made small, squawking sounds.

'What's it doing?' asked Gina nervously. 'What *is* that thing?'

'I think it's an automatic translator,' said Max 1. 'The Creature's working out our language, so it can talk to us.'

Gina looked relieved.

'Unless it's a weapon,' added Max 2, 'and the Creature's getting ready to kill us.'

Gina looked worried again.

Barney bared his teeth.

'I'm going to count to three, Creature,' he growled. 'One, two …'

The Creature finished pushing buttons and nodded, satisfied. Then it opened its mouth and began to speak.

As its mouth moved, sounds came from the gadget on its belt. Sounds that were words, spoken in a voice that sounded like the squawking of a bird.

'Tak my ta yo leeden,' the voice said.

The dogs looked at one another.

The Creature shook its head impatiently, fiddled with the buttons on the gadget and tried again, hunching its back against the rain. Its little blue teeth were chattering with cold.

'Take me to your leader,' the voice said, amid whistles and crackles.

Barney drew himself up to his full height.

'*I* am the leader,' he growled.

'Says who?' muttered Max 1, but Max 2 nudged him to be quiet.

'Greetings,' said the Creature to Barney. 'I am SR13, Official Planet Claimer, Second Grade, for the Alliance of Zern. I bear good news. Your planet has been chosen as a possible site for the next Alliance settlement. It is on a shortlist of eight.'

'Settlement?' Barney spluttered. 'You mean you want to *live* here? Well, you can't, and that's flat. This field is –'

'The claiming ceremony will be conducted in your native language, as per Guideline 3429(a) of the Revised Alliance Code,' the Creature went on, shivering and glancing at the sky. 'Please do not interrupt.'

It took a small silver stick from its belt. It planted the stick in the ground and carefully unrolled a flag that had been wound around its top. The flag was purple, with a bright orange square in the middle. Mavis eyed it with interest.

The Creature held up a piece of plastic covered in black writing, and turned to face the dogs. Rain dripped down its bald head as it began to read, standing very straight.

'In the presence of the leader and citizens of this planet, and according to Guidelines 217, 425 and 3429(a) of the Revised Alliance Code,' it squawked, 'I claim this planet for the Alliance of Zern.'

'You can't do that!' Gina exclaimed. She turned to the others. 'It can't do that, can it?' she demanded.

'Certainly not!' growled Barney. 'I've never heard anything so ridiculous in my –'

'Silence!' screeched the Creature. It flicked its finger and a blue light beamed out and struck Barney right between the eyes. Barney froze, his mouth gaping open.

Gina yelped in shock.

'The effect will wear off in time,' said the Creature, wincing at the noise. 'But be warned. Further interruption will not be tolerated.'

Furiously, it wiped its wet face. Then it began reading from the plastic again. 'Furthermore, by the power vested in me according to sub-section V15, paragraph 27(b) of the Revised Alliance Code …'

'I'm going inside,' said Max 2. 'This is even more boring than one of Barney's stories.'

'Be quiet and stay still,' snapped Max 1. 'I think it's getting annoyed. Do you want to get shot?'

'Pay attention, *please*!' shouted the Creature. It was now shivering so much that it could hardly hold the plastic, but it bravely went on reading. Its voice squawked on and on.

Max 2 pretended to snore.

'What are we going to do?' Scruffy whimpered. 'We can't just let it take over the Earth!'

Max 1 shrugged.

'It's not just a matter of the Earth,' said Gina. 'It's Barney's field!'

'And Mavis's,' said Scruffy quickly, afraid that Mavis would feel insulted.

But Mavis, who was quietly eating the flag, said nothing.

The rain grew heavier. The frogs sang even more loudly. The Creature's voice stopped. It could no longer see to read. Its long, thin fingers had gone dark blue with cold.

'It isn't dressed for this,' Max 2 pointed out.

At that, the Creature seemed to lose its temper. It threw the piece of plastic to the ground.

'What is this cold water that falls from the sky?' it demanded. 'And what is that terrible, harsh singing sound? Do these things never stop?'

'Oh, no,' said Max 2, nudging Max 1. 'Why do you think we wear fur coats? Why do you think our ears hang down? Oh, this is a miserable place. It's lucky you've come to take it off our hands.'

The Creature looked a little confused. It stood motionless in the rain, and shivered.

'Do you like your job, Creature?' Max 1 asked. 'It doesn't look much fun to me.'

'It is not supposed to be – fun,' the Creature said stiffly. 'It is my duty.'

At that moment, it turned and saw that the flag was gone. Its tiny mouth fell open.

'Where is the flag of the Alliance?' it squawked.

All the dogs put on innocent expressions. They were good at that. Especially Max 1 and Max 2.

'This – is – *intolerable*!' shouted the Creature. It frowned suspiciously at Mavis.

Mavis stared back, chewing lazily. The stubby end of the silver stick waggled on her bottom lip.

'Oh dear,' said Max 1. 'Looks like you'll have to start the claiming ceremony all over again, Creature. Never mind. We've got plenty of time. And we don't mind the rain, do we? Or the noise?'

'Oh, no,' called the other dogs in a chorus.

The Creature stamped its foot.

'Are you attempting to resist the might of the Alliance?' it shrieked, the gadget on its belt whistling and spluttering.

'We wouldn't think of such a thing,' said Max 1, yawning. 'If you want this planet, you can have it, as far as we're concerned.'

He shook himself violently, showering the Creature with hair and water.

The Creature shuddered in disgust, and began frantically brushing hairs from its soaked silver suit.

'Go and get another flag,' Mavis suggested hopefully.

The Creature threw up its hands in despair.

'I do not *have* another flag,' it wailed. 'They only gave me eight. I told them I needed one spare at least, but, oh, no! Too expensive, they said. And now, look. How can I claim a planet with no flag?'

'That's a problem, all right,' Max 1 and Max 2 agreed.

The Creature stared around helplessly. It looked tired, and seemed to Scruffy to be very near to tears. She felt quite sorry for it.

'You could just *pretend* you'd claimed this planet,' she said timidly. 'After all, you've got seven others to choose from for the settlement. And we won't tell.'

The Creature looked at her with desperate gratitude.

'You won't?' it asked. 'You promise?'

'Spit our deaths,' said the dogs – except for Barney, who was still frozen.

The Creature nodded quickly.

'All right, then,' it said. 'Thank you.'

Having made up its mind, it seemed to pull itself together. It wiped its face, and straightened its narrow shoulders.

'After all,' it muttered, looking around, 'who'd want to live here anyway?'

With that, it picked up the piece of plastic and scuttled back up into its ship.

The door slammed behind it, the lights went on.

The dogs flattened their ears as, with a sound like thunder, the ship rose from the grass and shot off into the clouds.

In moments, it had completely disappeared.

'So,' said Max 1 with satisfaction. 'That's that.'

Barney's jaws shut with a snap. He shook himself and stared around, confused.

'Don't worry,' Gina told him quickly. 'You've been having a little rest. The Creature's gone.'

Barney nodded vaguely.

'Oh, yes. I got rid of it quick smart,' he mumbled. 'Trespassers! They're all the same. Well, why are we standing here in the rain? Let's get inside. I'll put the heater on.'

He plodded off towards the house.

Max 1 and Max 2 looked at one another.

'We'll tell him tomorrow,' said Max 2. 'It wouldn't be a good plan to upset him now. We can't reach the heater switch at home.'

Scruffy yawned. The morning had been quite tiring. She needed a nice long nap. Then, perhaps, she'd have a treat. She might even dig up her special-occasion bone, if she could remember where she'd buried it.

After all, if saving the world wasn't a special occasion, what was?

5 Mavis Goes Mad

The next morning dawned fine and clear. After the Pets had left for the day, Scruffy, Gina, Max 1 and Max 2 went to Barney's front yard.

To their surprise, Barney wasn't there, and neither was Mavis.

This had only happened once before, when Barney had stayed up very late watching a horror movie marathon with his Pets. Barney had felt he couldn't let Bert and Alice watch alone, in case the movies became too scary. Bert, particularly, was very sensitive, Barney said.

The following morning, Alice and Bert had woken and gone out as usual, but Barney had slept in. That meant that Mavis had slept in, too. Mavis's shed was dark all day, and if Barney didn't call her she just happily assumed it was still night-time and stayed asleep, no matter what time it really was.

Perhaps, the dogs thought, Barney had stayed up late again.

They went around to the side of the house and Gina peeped cautiously through the door.

Barney's bed was empty.

'He must be in the field with Mavis,' said Gina.

Scruffy had been looking up at the trees, puzzled.

'Have you noticed there are no birds around this morning?' she said. 'Where are they all?'

'Off gossiping as usual, of course,' snorted Max 1.

'But nothing's happened here this morning to gossip *about*,' said Scruffy. 'And the birds don't know about the Creature From Outer Space yesterday, because they were all hiding away from the rain when it came.'

'Oh, you know how birds are,' said Max 2 disdainfully. 'They get excited about any little thing. One of them probably got a tough beetle for breakfast, or something. Who cares? Let's go and find Barney.'

The morning news was being called as the four dogs moved towards the back of the house. There wasn't a single item that was nearly as interesting as their own excitement of the day before, but of course they couldn't join the news and tell about that. It was a shame, but, as they had all agreed, a promise was a promise. Even when it was made to a Creature who smelt like petrol, flea soap and lizard.

Max 1 and Max 2 found this particularly annoying. They would have loved to boast about tricking the Creature From Outer Space into going away, because they thought it had been mainly their work.

'Scruffy helped too, you know,' Gina reminded them.

'And Mavis,' Scruffy added. 'Mavis ate the flag.'

Just at that moment, by a strange coincidence, a very loud, excited voice joined the news, and mentioned Mavis's name.

Amazed, the dogs all stopped to listen. And what they heard made their hair stand on end.

'Mavis of Dolan Street has gone mad!' cried the voice.

'She always *was* mad,' some unpleasant dog shouted in return. It was Garbage Guts, Scruffy was sure.

'Muzzle up, you two!' shouted another voice. 'There's nothing wrong with Mavis!' That was Deakin the Boxer. He was a loyal friend.

But then, suddenly, dozens of other dogs were

joining the chorus. It was true about Mavis, true! they were shouting. They'd just heard the news from the Dolan Street birds, who all told the same story.

'So that's where the birds are!' exclaimed Gina furiously. 'What do they think they're playing at?'

Together the friends ran to the end of the house and into the field at the back. And there they stopped dead.

Mavis was leaping around  the field. Wisps of straw were sticking in her hair, and her eyes were glazed. As the dogs watched, appalled, she lowered her head and charged wildly at something that no one else could see.

'Got you!' she shouted. Then she spun around and charged again, tossing her horns and laughing madly. 'Come on, then!' she called. 'Just try it! Ha, ha!'

Barney was slumped at the edge of the field, his head in his paws. The others rushed over to him, but he didn't look up.

'I can't make her stop,' he said mournfully. 'I don't think she even knows who I am.'

He groaned in dismay as Mavis sprang up and spun around in mid air, grinning fiercely.

'It's all I can do most days to get her to walk to the front of the house without falling asleep,' he said. 'It's years since she jumped over so much as a worm mound. And now look at her.'

'Weird,' agreed Max 1 and Max 2, gazing at Mavis in fascination.

'Barney, when did this start?' Gina cried in horror.

'She was like it when I came to wake her up, after Bert and Alice left,' said Barney. 'I think it must have come on her in the night. Her straw's barely been slept in.'

'But she must be exhausted!' Gina exclaimed. She raised her voice. 'Mavis!' she called. 'It's Gina. Stop jumping, Mavis! Come over here and talk to me!'

Mavis just gave a strange, high giggle and snapped at a passing butterfly before bounding on.

Scruffy felt cold. Was this the way *all* goats ended up? Was this, perhaps, what she herself had to look forward to, in the years to come?

She stumbled forward. Maybe Mavis would listen to her. After all, they had so much in common.

'Mavis!' she quavered. 'What's the matter? Can't you tell us? We really want to know.'

'No time!' shrieked Mavis. 'I have to fight them! They're everywhere! Can't you see?'

'What?' Scruffy shouted desperately.

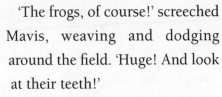

'The frogs, of course!' screeched Mavis, weaving and dodging around the field. 'Huge! And look at their teeth!'

'She's having daymares,' whispered Max 1. 'She's seeing things!'

'There are no frogs in the field, Mavis!' roared Barney. 'No frogs, I tell you! Stop this foolishness at once!'

'It's no good shouting at her,

Barney,' Gina murmured. 'We have to be kind, and very, very calm.'

She cleared her throat. 'We can't see any frogs, Mavis dear,' she called.

'Of course you can't!' bellowed Mavis. 'They're invisible!'

'If they're invisible, how does she know they're huge and have teeth?' muttered Max 2. 'And how does she know where they are?'

'Look out, here comes one of them now!' yelled Mavis. She ducked, then whirled around and butted the empty air.

'Got it!' she said, with satisfaction.

'Mad,' said Max 1.

Gina glared at him, then turned again to Mavis.

'There are no frogs over where we are, Mavis,' she called temptingly. 'It's quite safe here. Why don't you come and rest with us for a little while?'

Mavis glanced at her, and seemed to hesitate.

'Come on!' Gina called. 'You need a rest. And you've got rid of a lot of the frogs already, haven't you?'

Mavis nodded unwillingly, and licked her lips.

'There are lots left, though,' she said.

'Well, after your rest we'll help you fight the others,' said Gina.

Mavis thought for a moment, then nodded again. She started backing towards them, very, very slowly.

'I'm not going out there chasing invisible giant frogs, Gina,' said Max 1. 'What if the birds come back and see us? They'll tell everyone *we've* gone loopy, too.'

'Don't be so *selfish*!' Gina hissed. 'Don't you want to help Mavis?'

'Acting as mad as she does won't help her,' Max 1 said. 'And I won't do it, whatever you say.'

His brother was watching Mavis as she backed towards them. She was looking right and left, occasionally snapping her jaws and tossing her horns at invisible enemies.

'They shoot mad dogs, you know,' he said. 'I saw a movie about that, once. Is she foaming at the mouth?'

Max 1 craned his neck to see. 'I don't think so,' he said.

'There'll be no talk of foaming or shooting here!' growled Barney. 'We have to try to find out what's wrong with Mavis and fix it. Dogs don't just start seeing invisible frogs for no reason! Or no dogs *I've* ever heard of.'

'But Mavis *isn't* a dog!' Scruffy burst out. 'She's a goat!'

All the others turned on her, horrified.

'Don't say that!' exclaimed Gina, her eyes on Mavis. 'She might hear you!'

'But don't you see?' Scruffy demanded in a trembling voice. 'Maybe she's started to *suspect*. Maybe it was something the birds said. About her horns, for example. She could be having an identity crisis.'

Barney gritted his teeth. 'If that's the case, all this is my fault,' he muttered.

'You mustn't blame yourself, Barney,' said Gina. 'You did your best, and –'

Mavis squealed and suddenly picked up speed.

'Watch out!' yelled Max 1. He grabbed his brother and pulled him aside just as Mavis leaped backwards, landing with a thump where they'd been standing.

'That was a near thing,' gasped Max 2.

'It certainly was,' Mavis agreed, her eyes rolling. 'That one nearly got me.'

The dogs looked at one another nervously.

'You're quite safe now, Mavis dear,' said Gina, trying to remember how the doctors on 'Dog Hospital' treated disturbed patients. 'Lie down. Tell us what's troubling you.'

Shivering, Mavis collapsed on the grass.

'She should be lying on a couch,' said Max 1.

'It doesn't matter where she lies,' snapped Barney. He bent over Mavis and patted her shoulder awkwardly.

'What's the problem, Mavis?' he asked. 'Tell old Barney. Are you having a crisis?'

Mavis laughed piercingly. 'Of course I am!' she cackled. 'What would *you* call being attacked by giant frogs? A picnic?'

Gina frowned and shook her head at Barney.

'Close your eyes now, Mavis,' she said soothingly. 'Just relax. We're your friends. You're safe. We'll protect you.'

Mavis stared wildly for a moment, then suddenly yawned and closed her eyes. In moments she was fast asleep.

Everyone breathed a sigh of relief.

'She might be suffering from stress,' Gina whispered.

'*Stress*?' Max 1 jeered. 'Mavis is the least stressed animal I know! *Stones* suffer more stress than Mavis.'

'That's not true,' said Scruffy, rushing to Mavis's defence. 'The birds stress her, when they sit on her head. She's worried about her tree. And the frogs upset her, too, with their noise. I'm sure that's why she's having daymares about them now. She could probably hear them having a party in the night.'

'They have a party *every* night,' Barney pointed out irritably. 'And she's never gone mad before.'

'That's true.' Scruffy considered that for a moment. 'So – what was different about last night?'

They all thought carefully. But no one could think of anything.

'I went to bed early,' said Barney. 'That saving the world business yesterday was quite tiring, I found.'

'I don't see how it could have made *you* tired, Barney,' scoffed Max 1. 'You were zapped! You slept through most of it. You slept through that Creature's incredibly boring speech. You slept through Mavis eating the flag. You slept through –'

'*What?*' Barney interrupted, leaning forward urgently. '*What* did you say? *What* did Mavis eat?'

'The Creature's flag,' said Max 1 in surprise. 'Mavis liked the look of it, and so she –'

'Oh, Barney!' sighed Gina, clasping her paws. 'Do you think that's it?'

Barney leaped to his feet, his eyes gleaming.

'Of course that's it!' he growled. 'Mavis has a strong stomach, as everyone knows. But eating a flag from Outer Space – why, who knows what horrible alien chemicals it had in it! Not to mention horrible alien artificial colourings and flavourings. No wonder it's given her daymares!'

'So – so what do we do?' Scruffy stammered.

'Nothing,' said Barney firmly, looking down at the soundly sleeping Mavis. 'Despite everything, I have perfect faith in Mavis's stomach. I've seen that stomach digest things you wouldn't believe. And it will cope with this, I'm sure of it. All it needs is time.'

Barney was right. The dogs watched over Mavis as she slept on and on. She slept till the sun was high in the sky. And when she woke, she was the old Mavis again. A little bit weak. A little bit trembly. But not even the littlest bit mad.

The Maxes were clearly rather disappointed. They'd enjoyed the excitement. But everyone else was thrilled to have Mavis in her senses again.

'Oh, Mavis,' cried Gina, hugging her.

'Welcome back!' shouted Scruffy.

'Have I been somewhere?' asked Mavis. She struggled to get up, and licked her lips.

'I'm hungry,' she said.

'Stay right where you are,' said Barney sternly, pushing her back down onto the grass. 'You are to lie down for the rest of the day, Mavis, and you are to eat nothing but what I bring you. Some oat-and-molasses cake, and a nice fresh thistle or two, for now, I think. I'm not going through *that* again.'

'Through what again?' asked Mavis. But not very loudly. If Barney was willing to bring her oat-and-molasses cake, of which she was very fond, she wasn't going to argue.

And besides, she'd always wanted breakfast in bed.

6 A Terrible Shock

Early the next morning, Scruffy's Petlings, Hannah and Reuben, wanted to play ball in the yard.

Now, normally Scruffy was very happy to play with the Petlings, but the crack of dawn, in her opinion, was not the right time for running around. It was a time for stretching, yawning and trying to remember your dreams so you could tell your friends about them, even if they didn't want to listen.

This morning, especially, she would have liked to sleep in. She had really been very worried about Mavis the day before, and worry is always tiring.

But Scruffy was a kind dog, and very fond of her Pets. She didn't want to disappoint Hannah and

Reuben. So after they had called her for the third time, she climbed down from the couch where she always spent the second half of the night, and went outside to join them.

She was rather surprised – and a tiny bit annoyed, actually – to find that the Petlings lost interest in the ball game very quickly. After the first few throws, in fact, their mother, Julie, called them and they started to wander off towards the house again.

Gently but firmly, Scruffy called them back. She knew that it wasn't a good idea to let Pets fall into

bad habits. If she let them get away with rousing her early for no reason, they might do the same thing the next day, and the next. And that would never do.

But instead of obeying her call, Reuben very

cheekily threw the ball high in the air and ran to the back door, with Hannah close behind him.

The morning sun dazzled Scruffy's eyes. She couldn't see the ball against the sky at all. She had no idea where it was – until it fell down and bounced, hard, on her head.

For a few seconds Scruffy saw tiny pinpoints of light dancing before her eyes.

She shook her head and sat down carefully on the grass. She felt dizzy, and a bit sick.

For a while she stayed quite still. Then, when the worst of the unpleasant feelings had passed, she picked up the ball and walked slowly back to the house.

She felt confused, and rather upset.

She knew that Reuben hadn't meant the ball to fall on her head. And she didn't blame him, or Hannah, for not rushing to comfort her. Neither of them realised she'd been hurt. They were both inside by the time the ball fell.

But why had they disturbed her in the first place, if they hadn't really wanted to play? A suspicious dog might wonder if the whole game had just been an excuse to get her outside.

That's what Max 1 and Max 2 would think, Scruffy said to herself, as she put the ball back in its place in the laundry. But why would my Petlings *do* such a thing?

She sighed as she walked on through the kitchen.

Hannah and Reuben were sitting there, having their breakfast. They called out to Scruffy, but she didn't stop.

For one thing, she had to show them that she was displeased with their behaviour outside. For another, she wanted nothing more than to get back on her couch and rest her aching head.

She reached the family room and went over to the corner where her couch was.

And – the couch was gone!

Scruffy blinked. She couldn't believe it. There, where the couch had always been, she saw only a patch of carpet, some balls of fluff, a sprinkling of sweet wrappers, an odd sock and a dog treat she remembered hiding under one of the cushions a few months earlier.

The shock was so great that for a moment Scruffy didn't know what to do. She went and lay down on the empty patch of carpet, half thinking that perhaps, if she did that, the couch would appear again. But of course it didn't.

After a while she became aware that her Pets had started running around, shouting at each other, falling over and losing things. This meant that they were getting ready to leave for the day.

None of them seemed to have noticed that the couch had disappeared. Scruffy clambered to her feet and tried to show them what had happened. But they were too over-excited to take any notice.

She followed them outside, still trying to explain, but it was hopeless. They just wouldn't listen.

They said goodbye to her very lovingly, as always. Then, as they ran to their cars, which, strangely, were parked in the street this morning, instead of in the driveway, Scruffy saw an astounding sight.

Her couch was *on the grass outside the fence*!

The Pets didn't look surprised to see it there. Reuben actually patted it as he got into the car. Patted it as he had patted Scruffy when he left. As if he was saying goodbye!

At that moment, Scruffy realised that the Pets had moved her couch out into the street while she was in the back yard.

Why had they done that?

Doors slammed, and the cars drove away. Scruffy was left alone, looking out through the bars of the fence.

The sweet, familiar smell of the couch drifted into her nose, beckoning to her. But she couldn't get out. She couldn't reach it.

'Scruffy!'

Gina was pressing against the side fence, calling urgently. Scruffy walked slowly over to her.

'You're moving away!' Gina wailed. 'Why didn't you *tell* us?' She knew that the couch was Scruffy's bed. She had visited Scruffy's house many times, as they were next-door neighbours.

'I'm not going anywhere,' said Scruffy, feeling dazed. 'At least, I don't think so.'

Gina's Pet, Caroline, was watering the garden, which she always did just before leaving for the day. The dogs watched as Caroline glanced at the couch standing by the road. She didn't seem at all surprised.

How strange Pets are! thought Scruffy. They live in a world all their own.

'Then what's happening? Why is your bed in the street?' asked Gina.

Scruffy shook her head helplessly. She just didn't know.

$\bowtie\!\!\!\bowtie\!\!\!\bowtie$

After Caroline left, Scruffy and Gina went together to Barney's front yard.

All the others were already there.

It wasn't a happy group this morning. The Maxes were both glowering, and Barney was fuming, because earlier that morning some birds had left a dead worm in his food bowl as a joke.

'They hid in the trees and watched me smell it,' he raged, baring his teeth. 'Then they had the cheek to shout out to me that it was a baby sausage. They were actually hoping I'd eat it, so they could rush off and spread the word!'

'They rushed off anyway, and spread the word that you *nearly* ate it,' said Max 1. 'You heard the news. The whole neighbourhood's laughing.'

'As if it wasn't laughing already,' Barney muttered. 'What with that shameful Garbage Guts affair, and Mavis's – little illness.'

'Never mind about my illness. You shouldn't even have *sniffed* at that worm, Barney,' said Mavis, chewing a stick gloomily. 'Not after that insect business.'

Max 2 ground his teeth in anger. 'It's so *embarrassing*! Imagine what the Danger Corner Rottweilers are saying!'

'Who cares what they're saying?' said Gina sharply.

'*I* care!' said Max 2. 'These days we're the joke of the neighbourhood. Us! Who saved the world single-pawed!'

His brother nodded violently.

'It's completely unfair!' he agreed. 'Instead of understanding that we're heroes, and praising us and thanking us and bringing us presents, everyone thinks we're losing our grip!'

'I'm not surprised,' said Barney heavily. 'Things are getting very lax around here.'

Scruffy's heart sank as he turned to her, frowning.

'What are you thinking of, young Scruffy, letting

your Pets move the furniture into the street?' he demanded. 'What do you think the birds are going to make of that, eh?'

Scruffy felt her ears droop. A large lump seemed to have appeared in her throat.

'It's not just furniture,' she said in a small voice. 'It's my bed!'

Mavis gasped, and the end of the stick fell off her bottom lip and onto the ground. The Maxes squeaked in amazement. Barney looked first astounded, then disapproving.

'You sleep on a *couch*?' he exclaimed. 'But that's not very good for your back, is it? Couches are all very well for naps. But for proper sleeping, dogs need a good firm surface.'

'Oh, I start *off* on a good firm surface,' Scruffy said hastily. 'My bed in the laundry is *very* firm. But as the night goes on, I like to move to the couch. It's much cosier.'

'That's right,' Max 1 and Max 2 agreed. 'We do the same thing at our place when we can, but John and Sal keep forgetting to leave the living room door open.'

'Caroline seems to think *my* couch belongs to *her*,' said Gina, smiling fondly. 'Do you know …'

Scruffy felt a twinge of resentment. This was a crisis. Surely, just for once, Gina could resist bringing

Caroline's cute ways into the conversation.

But no such luck.

'… Do you know that sometimes she actually tries to stop me getting onto it, so she can have it all to herself!' Gina went on.

Max 1, Max 2 and Mavis laughed, but Barney frowned.

'You spoil that Pet of yours, Gina,' he said. 'One day you'll be sorry. Still, I've said it once, and I'll say it again – there was none of this soft sleeping on couches when I was a pup. Why, I'd never even seen a *blanket* till I came here to live. I slept on a wooden floor. Have I ever told you that?'

'Many times,' groaned Max 1.

'A wooden floor with sharp nails sticking out of it, Barney?' asked Max 2 cheekily.

'It did have nails, yes,' said Barney, with dignity. 'Not particularly sharp, but –'

'Not *sharp*?' exclaimed Max 2. 'Well, what are you complaining about? Why, I once knew a dog who …'

Suddenly Scruffy couldn't stand it any longer. Her friends were talking about things that didn't matter at all, while her couch was standing outside, practically on the road, where any thief could steal it.

As Max 2 went on making fun of Barney, she crept away.

7 Facing the Future

At home, Scruffy wandered around the house, unable to relax. After a while she found herself in front of the long mirror in the hall. She glanced at her reflection out of habit, then froze.

What was wrong with the fur on her head? It was standing up slightly, just on one side, beside her left ear.

She looked more closely, then raised a paw to try to smooth the fur down. But the fur wouldn't flatten, because underneath it there was a small, tender lump.

Scruffy's heart gave a tremendous leap.

Carefully she checked the other side of her head. So far, there was no matching lump there, but she knew that it wouldn't be long before it appeared.

Horns were beginning to grow. Here was the final proof.

She was a goat.

Stunned, Scruffy wandered outside again, trying to take it all in.

She had suspected her goatness for a long time – ever since she first realised how much she resembled Mavis. All the same, now that she knew it for sure, she found it strangely hard to accept.

Growing up was like that, no doubt.

She went to the gate and stared out at her couch standing forlornly beside the road. Now, of course, she understood why it was there.

Her Pets had seen the change in her before she had seen it herself. As Barney and Gina always said, Pets had amazing instincts.

Zac, Julie, Hannah and Reuben had realised that Scruffy was a goat, and naturally thought she would not want to live in the house with them any longer. They were getting ready to move her bed across the road and into Mavis's field.

Just then, a truck came down Dolan Street and

stopped right outside Scruffy's house. Two strange, suspicious-looking Pets jumped out. They threw open the back doors of the truck, then together they picked up the couch.

'No!' Scruffy shouted. 'That's mine!'

She hurled herself against the gate, but the Pets barely looked at her. They dragged the couch into the truck and shut the doors again.

'Stop, thief! Help!' Scruffy called desperately.

Sunny and Tiger answered, and so did Mattie the Poodle, but they were too far away to be of any use.

'Gina, Mavis, Barney, Max!' yelled Scruffy. But she knew, even as she called, that it was hopeless.

By now her friends would be inside Barney's house, watching 'Dog Hospital'. With the volume turned up to drown out the Maxes' arguing, they'd never hear her.

Scruffy watched helplessly as the truck turned and rumbled back up the hill, taking her couch with it. When it was out of sight, she flopped down beside the gate, whimpering in despair.

Now what was going to happen? Now she had no bed!

After a while she managed to pull herself together. She told herself that this was no way for a goat to behave. Goats were strong, calm and brave. Mavis

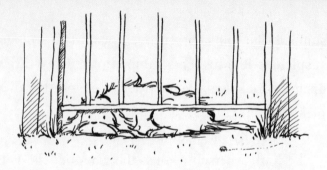

would never lie around crying because things hadn't worked out the way she wanted them to.

Scruffy knew that, even if she herself was still only a small goat, she had to live up to Mavis's example.

She had a drink of water, then crawled through the side fence into Gina's garden. From there she hurried into the frogs' ground and made her way back into Barney's place.

She could hear the sounds of television and raised voices floating through the door, but she didn't go into the house. Instead, she went along the side to the field at the back. She had never been there alone before, but she knew that Barney and Mavis wouldn't mind if she looked around. After all, it was to be her home from now on.

The field was large and empty, except for Mavis's shed. It looked rather dreary.

A tree will certainly improve it, Scruffy thought. If Mavis ever makes up her mind which tree to have.

There didn't seem to be any birds around for the

moment, but the frogs in the swampy ground were calling out loudly to one another. Their voices seemed to echo across the barren field.

Scruffy couldn't understand a word. She wondered if they were talking about her. Had they noticed the beginning of the horn?

Flattening her ears to shut out the sound, she went over to the fence at the other side of the field and peered through the wire.

Next door, in the Maxes' yard, there was a lot of grass, a tumbledown old shed, a half-dug vegetable garden and a clothesline. Not much of a view. Nothing like Gina's pretty flower garden, which Caroline tended so lovingly. Also, the back of the Maxes' house was rather shabby, its dull white boards peeling in places. Gina's was painted a very nice pink, at the back as well as the front.

Well, it can't be helped, Scruffy told herself. The Maxes are going to be my neighbours from now on. I'll just have to get used to it.

Despite all her resolutions to be brave, her ears drooped.

She sighed and went on down to the shed. Stopping at the doorway, she peered in.

The shed was very dim, and the floor was heaped with straw. There wasn't much space. Scruffy didn't think her couch would have fitted in, even if she still had it.

She looked around. Her bed from the laundry could probably fit in the darkest corner, she decided. But her food and water bowls would have to stay outside.

For the first time, Scruffy wondered if Mavis would mind sharing. It would be very cramped, with two in the shed.

Just then she heard a sound and saw that Mavis was coming towards her. 'Dog Hospital' must have finished.

Scruffy licked her lips. She was determined to keep up a brave face.

'How was the show?' she asked, trying to seem casual.

'Not bad,' said Mavis. Her voice was rather muffled because she was chewing what seemed to be the remains of a cardboard box. 'Lucas has realised he's in love with Jessica. And a three-legged Pekingese got hit by a car.'

'Was it badly hurt?' Scruffy asked, keeping the conversation going.

'I don't remember,' Mavis said vaguely. 'I think I had a little nap. What are you doing here?'

'Just looking at your room,' said Scruffy. 'You don't mind, do you?'

'Not at all,' said Mavis. She looked around her shed with pride. 'Nice place, isn't it? Nothing like straw for bedding, I always say. The beauty of it is, if you get hungry in the night, you can eat it.'

'That must be handy,' Scruffy murmured. 'But the shed – it's not terribly big, is it?'

Mavis stared at her. 'It's quite big enough for me,' she said, rather huffily.

'Oh, of course!' Scruffy babbled. 'I just meant – it would be a very tight squeeze for two. If you ever – I mean – if you ever got a flatmate.'

Mavis snorted. 'What would I want with a flatmate?' she demanded.

'I like my privacy far too much for *that*, thank you very much!'

Scruffy nodded, and tried to smile. Her heart felt as though it had sunk to her toes.

This was awful! Was she going to have to sleep in the open field?

Then she heard Gina calling her name. Barney was

calling, too. And Max 1 and Max 2 were joining in.

'Oh,' said Mavis, chewing. 'I forgot. Everyone's looking for you. That was why I came out here in the first place. One of your Pets has come home again. Julie, I think it is.'

'What?' Her heart beating very fast, Scruffy dashed away.

Why would Julie have come back so soon? She must have been hurt in some way. Or perhaps she had suddenly fallen ill.

Scruffy didn't even look up until she had scrambled into her own front garden. Then she stopped, panting and amazed.

Julie, looking perfectly healthy, was standing at the open door. A truck, bigger and shinier than the one that had taken the couch away, was parked in the driveway. Two Pets, complete strangers, were pulling something out of the back of the truck.

It was a new couch! It was beautiful, big and very comfortable looking, with plump, squashy cushions.

Astounded, Scruffy watched as the two Pets carried the couch inside, carefully easing it through the door. She followed and saw Julie showing them where to put it.

Right where the old couch used to be.

'So you see, they'd planned it all between them, to give me a surprise,' Scruffy said to her friends later. 'They must have decided that the old couch was getting too shabby for me to sleep on. So they got me a new one.'

'What a present!' Max 1 said enviously.

'In my day,' growled Barney, 'dogs only got presents on their birthdays and at Christmas. And even then it was just a bone or a bag of dog treats or something. Once, I only got a bar of flea soap. *And* I was grateful. Couches, indeed! I don't know what the world's coming to.'

'I'll bet Julie was pleased at how surprised you were,' said Gina, very glad that her friend was happy again.

Scruffy laughed. 'She was thrilled. She kept showing me how comfortable the couch is, and making jokes about how it's so good and new that I mustn't sit on it, and so on. She's got a wonderful sense of humour – almost doglike, sometimes.'

'Have you tried it out yet?' asked Max 2.

'Oh, yes,' Scruffy said. 'As soon as Julie left. It's marvellous. There's only one thing – it doesn't smell quite as good as my old couch.'

'Ah, well, it's very new,' said Gina kindly. 'New things always smell different.'

'Oh, yes. As Old Buster used to say, couches are like fine bones,' rumbled Barney. 'They improve with time. You'll just have to wear it in, young dog. Put a bit of work into it.'

Scruffy nodded. 'I might go and put a bit of work into it now,' she said.

☙❦❧

Scruffy trotted home and let herself into the house through her special door. Then, before going to the new couch, she went to look in the mirror in the hall. After all, her worries weren't over yet.

To her surprise, the fur on her head seemed to be lying quite neatly again.

Carefully she felt the place with her paw.

Yes, there was no doubt about it. The lump had gone down. The place where the horn had been growing was a little tender to touch, but that was all. And on the other side there was still no sign of swelling at all.

It had all been a false alarm! No doubt the horns would grow, eventually. But for now, at least, her goatness was still hidden, and there was to be no problem about where to live.

Or where to sleep. Scruffy yawned, heading for the family room.

As she jumped up onto her splendid new couch,

and stretched out fully on its plump softness, another thought occurred to her.

This couch was not only more comfortable than the old one, but larger, too. Much larger than she really needed.

It was really very big indeed. Why, it was big enough for …

And then, at that moment, Scruffy realised something wonderful.

A great wave of thankfulness and pleasure rolled over her, warming her heart.

At last she understood everything.

At last she realised just how much her Pets loved her, and how touchingly they had tried to plan for the future.

They had done their best to make sure that she would never, ever want to leave them.

For *this* couch, unlike the old one, was plenty big enough, *more* than big enough, for a fully grown goat.

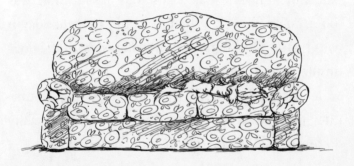

8 The Haunting

The Dolan Street Pets did not go out in their cars every morning. Every Sixth and Seventh Day, without fail, they all put on different clothes and stayed at home to work around the houses, cut the grass, and spend time with the dogs.

'It's amazing how they know,' Gina often said affectionately. But Max 1 and Max 2 said there was no mystery about it. The Pets could tell what day it was by the TV programs they watched with the dogs in the evenings.

It was fun having the Pets around, and of course they deserved a bit of attention. All Pets, especially Petlings, need plenty of affection and exercise.

Also, as Barney pointed out, it was good to encourage them to tidy up and, in particular, to cut the grass. Long grass was not as comfortable as trimmed grass, he had found, and, besides, it attracted snails.

Looking after the Pets took a lot of time and energy, and while they were home the dogs rarely had the chance to get together and relax. So when Barney called Scruffy, Gina and the Maxes to a meeting in the field early one Seventh Day evening, Scruffy knew that the matter was urgent.

She slipped into Gina's house, and she and Gina hurried to the field together. Both of them thought the meeting would be something to do with the untrue stories that were still being called out about them on the news.

This very morning, though Seventh Day news was usually brief, there had been a sly remark about Scruffy's couch. Someone claimed to have heard that the Dolan Street dogs were having to sell their beds for food, and that they were desperate.

Mattie the Poodle had actually called in at Scruffy's house during the day, to drop off a small parcel of bones. Always tactful, she had told Scruffy, in her charming French accent, that she was trying to lose weight, so didn't want the bones herself.

'I leave zem wiz you. You will share wiz zee ozzers, *non*?' she had said casually. 'If zey feel like a snack.'

Scruffy hadn't known quite what to say. It would have been rude to reject the present, but she knew that Mattie was only giving it because she had heard that the Dolan Street dogs were starving.

'We really have enough food, you know, Mattie,' she said at last. 'That story on the news wasn't true.'

'Of course it was not!' cried Mattie at once, waving her paw. 'No, no! As if such a tale could be true! I did not believe it for a moment! But still, zose young Maxes always 'ave room for more, *non*? And you, too, *ma chère* Scruffy.'

She tossed her ears back, looking everywhere but straight into Scruffy's eyes. 'And so? I bring zee bones,' she went on brightly. 'Ozzerwise, zey go into zee garbage, do zey not? What waste! I could not bear it!'

She was trying to protect Scruffy's pride, but clearly she still believed the story. In the end, Scruffy had taken the bones. What else could she do?

When Gina and Scruffy arrived in the field, they found Barney sitting, shoulders hunched, and Mavis standing behind him, looking very grave.

To the visitors' surprise, Barney did not even greet them, or turn around. He was staring fixedly through the wire fence into the Maxes' back yard.

As the others watched, he looked slowly up at the rising moon and sighed deeply.

'What is it?' Gina whispered to Mavis, very concerned.

Mavis shook her head. 'Wait,' she whispered back.

A few moments later, Max 1 and Max 2 came pounding towards them.

'We can't stay long,' Max 1 gabbled. 'We're on duty. John's lit the barbecue, and by the smell of it, there's chicken.'

'Don't mention that word!' Barney had swung around and was glaring at them.

The Maxes stared back at him, stunned.

'How – *could* – you?' Barney growled.

'What?' demanded Max 1.

'How *could* you let your Pets do … *that*?' snarled Barney.

He jerked his head towards Max 1 and Max 2's yard, where spades, a rake, a wheelbarrow and a roll of wire stood beside the tumbledown shed at the bottom of the garden.

Max 1 rolled his eyes. 'What are you getting your tail in a knot about now, Barney,' he sighed. 'They're just cleaning up the old hen house.'

'They don't mind,' Max 2 added. 'They've been

messing about there all day, getting dirty and smelly. They love it! Why shouldn't we let them have a bit of fun?'

Barney licked his lips. Then he nodded slowly.

'I apologise,' he said. 'I shouldn't have snapped at you. How were you to know?'

'Know what?' demanded Max 1.

'That is no ordinary hen house,' muttered Barney.

'What are you talking about?' Max 2 was dancing with impatience, anxious to be gone.

Barney closed his eyes, breathing deeply.

Long moments passed. The Maxes fidgeted. Gina and Scruffy waited nervously. Mavis stood rigidly, staring at the sky.

At last Barney's eyes opened again. Scruffy shivered as she saw that they seemed darker, larger. They were like deep pools of dread. And when Barney spoke, his voice was flat and cold.

'That is no ordinary hen house,' he repeated. 'That hen house is – haunted!'

Scruffy squeaked, and shrank closer to Gina. But Max 1 and Max 2 were not impressed. They sniggered and nudged one another.

Barney turned away from them and looked up at the sky. It was darker now. The moon was a perfect circle, white and glowing.

'It all began long, long ago,' Barney went on, still in that same low, dead voice. 'Before I was born. I heard the story from Old Buster, may his bones rest in peace.'

'Oh, not Old Buster again,' Max 1 muttered. But Barney pretended not to hear.

'Old Buster, as I may have told you once or twice, taught me everything I know. He was a fine dog. Ah, yes. They don't make dogs like Old Buster any more.'

He bowed his head, and for a moment was silent. Then he began to speak again.

'The hen house was already ancient when Old Buster himself was a pup – Young Buster he was known as in those days, of course –'

'You don't say!' yawned Max 2. Gina gave him a warning look.

Barney raised his voice slightly.

'And in that hen house lived Speckles – the most enormous, the most terrible, the most evil hen the world had ever seen.'

'Evil?' quavered Scruffy. She could feel the fur standing up on the back of her neck and looked quickly to see if Mavis's was doing the same. Unfortunately,

the light had dimmed so much she couldn't tell.

'Evil!' Barney repeated. 'Proud, wild – and … vicious. She lived in that great hen house all alone, for all the other hens had gone long ago. Driven off, Buster thought, or worse …'

He paused, to let that thought sink in.

'Speckles' Pet, who was very old, was totally in her power. She had trained him to bring her food in the morning and to open her door in mid-afternoon so that she was free to roam the yard. Buster said he would never forget how her eyes gleamed with hatred as she pecked at him through the fence wire.'

The shadows seemed to be closing in. Gina felt for Scruffy's paw as Barney went on.

'At night in her shed Speckles would cackle to herself, muttering curses and spells and scuffling in the straw. Then she would begin to screech aloud.

'"I've outlived them all," she would cry. "Now this is mine, all mine! And one day I shall lay an egg the like of which the world has never seen! And it will reign in my place, the greatest and most powerful egg of all time!"'

Barney drew a deep, shuddering breath.

'Then she would laugh, horribly, on and on,' he whispered. 'That laughter haunted Buster's dreams long after – IT – happened.'

It was growing darker. The hen house was just a black shape humped against the sky. But it seemed to the dogs that they could hear, drifting on the breeze, the small, sighing sound of something moving behind the wire.

'After *what* happened? Get on with it!' Max 1 was trying to sound unconcerned, but his voice was much higher than usual.

'Speckles, like her Pet, was very, very old,' said Barney. 'She had not laid an egg for years. But one night – the night of the full moon, as it is tonight – there was a weird, high cackling from the hen house.

'Buster sprang out of bed, ran down here and hurried to the fence. And so it was that he saw what happened next. He saw Speckles, running around the hen house yard, flapping her wings and screeching, "I did it! I did it! Egg! Egg! Egg!".

She flung her head back and looked at the moon, laughing, her eyes glittering with triumph. Then, suddenly, at that exact moment, she toppled backwards, stone dead.'

Max 1, Max 2, Gina and Scruffy gasped.

Barney nodded slowly. Despite his worries, he seemed pleased at the effect of his story. He didn't always have such success.

Max 2 was the first to recover.

'How did Old Buster know she was dead?' he demanded. 'She might just have been asleep.'

Barney looked at him with disdain.

'Hens do not usually sleep on their backs with their feet in the air,' he said. 'But just to make sure Buster crouched by the fence all night. Speckles never moved. In the morning, her Pet came to bring her food, and found her. She was stiff and cold. Buster watched as, slowly, the Pet dug a hole and buried her *in the hen house yard.*'

'Why did he do that?' whispered Gina.

'Buster always thought it was because the Pet knew that was what Speckles would have wanted,' said Barney. 'It was *her* hen house. It would always be hers.'

'Oh, garbage and gristle!' exploded Max 1. 'It was probably because he couldn't be bothered carrying her outside!'

'Sneer if you will, little dog,' said Barney solemnly. 'But the fact remains that after he had buried Speckles, the Pet went into the hen house, and came out with an enormous speckled egg. He carried it respectfully up to the house, and that was the last Buster ever saw of it. But often, after that, on full moon nights, Buster would hear a wailing cackle from the deserted hen house.

'"Where is my egg?" a ghostly voice would cry. "Give me back my egg!" And Buster knew that, if he looked, he would see a pale, flickering shape drifting

around the hen house yard. Speckles. Searching, searching ...'

Barney's voice trailed off.

'That's just a story. Buster was making it up to scare you – the old windbag,' Max 2 said weakly. 'We've never seen anything like that. Or heard anything like that either.'

He spun round to Max 1. 'Have we?' he demanded.

'No,' murmured Max 1. But he didn't sound very sure.

'When Speckles' Pet died, just before I came here, the haunting ceased,' said Barney heavily. 'But Old Buster knew that the danger wasn't past. He warned me that Speckles was only resting. Gathering strength. Waiting her time.' He took a deep breath. 'And now that time has come. The hen of all evil has found new servants to do her will.'

He lifted his chin, fighting for control. 'Your Pets, Max 1 and Max 2, have fallen into Speckles' power,' he growled. 'They are following her ghastly, ghostly orders. They are making the hen house ready … for her return.'

Gina gave a long, low moan. Scruffy whimpered in terror. The Maxes drew closer together.

'John and Sal can't be in Speckles' power,' Max 1 yelped. 'We would have noticed.'

Mavis stirred, and spoke for the first time.

'If they are *not* in her power,' she said in a tight voice, '*why did they clean up the hen house*?'

There was no answer to that. And at that moment everyone knew that they, their Pets, and the whole Dolan Street way of life, were threatened.

9 Full Moon Night

'What are we going to do?' Max 2 whispered.

'We must destroy the source of Speckles' power.
Destroy it completely,' said Barney.

'How?' Gina cried. Nothing she had ever seen on
'Dog Hospital' had prepared her for this.

'Blow up the hen house!' yelled Max 1, cheering
up instantly.

'Burn down the hen house!' shouted Max 2, at the
same moment.

Barney sighed. 'You two watch far too much
television,' he said. 'Dolan Street is not Chicago.
But you're right about one thing. The hen house is
certainly the problem. I've thought long and hard on

what to do about it. And so has Mavis – not that she came up with anything.'

'I thought of eating it,' said Mavis indignantly.

Barney shook his head. His eyes had grown clearer, and his lips were firm. Now that his terrible story had been told, he was more himself again.

'The hen house need not be destroyed,' he announced. 'Instead, it must be cleansed.'

'But John and Sal have already done that!' Max 1 objected.

'Cleaning a place up is not at all the same as cleansing it of evil,' Barney said patiently. 'As anyone who has seen *Return of the Living Dead* knows –'

'And he says *we* watch too much television,' Max 2 muttered.

'As anyone who has seen *any* of the fine films on this subject knows,' Barney went on, ignoring the interruption, 'holy water is the best possible thing for cleansing. It never fails.'

'Do we *have* any holy water?' asked Scruffy hopefully.

'As it happens, no,' said Barney. 'Or, at least, if we do, I don't know where it is, and neither does Mavis. But we do have *hose* water.'

'*Hose* water?' echoed Scruffy, bewildered.

Barney nodded solemnly. 'Yes. According to my calculations, hose water is probably only half as powerful as the real thing. So all we have to do is use *twice as much*!'

'Oh, Barney, you're so clever!' Gina gasped.

'*I* helped,' Mavis protested. '*I* said I didn't know where any holy water was.'

'You're clever too, Mavis,' said Scruffy loyally.

The Maxes had begun jumping around in excitement.

'Let's do it, then!' Max 1 exclaimed. 'We've got a long hose next door. A *very* long hose. If we all work together –'

'We can't do it *now*,' Barney interrupted. 'What are you thinking of? These things are always done at midnight.'

'It would be better if we waited till the Pets are asleep, anyway, wouldn't it?' Scruffy put in timidly. 'If John and Sal see us doing the cleansing they might try to stop us – being in Speckles' power and everything.'

'And the others, dear things, won't understand what we're doing,' Gina agreed. 'They'll get all upset. You know how excitable they are.'

So the plan was made.

It was agreed that the dogs would all go back to their homes and act as normally as possible.

Barney thought that Max 1 and Max 2, especially, would find it very hard to do this, so it was decided that they would all pretend to be tired and go to bed early. To make sure that Speckles was not alerted to their plans, even Mavis would not stir until just before midnight, when they would all creep out and meet by the tap in the Maxes' back yard.

Everyone followed the plan exactly. Even when a van came down Dolan Street, turned around and stopped outside the Maxes' house, even when John and Sal went outside to greet the driver, no one stirred.

But Max 1 and Max 2 whispered together, eaten up with curiosity. And Barney tossed and turned on his blanket next door, wondering if a van counted as part of the Sausage Appearing Spell, and if he was missing out on the chance of a lifetime.

Just before midnight, all the dogs crept into Max 1 and Max 2's back yard. Scruffy and Gina were a little bit late, because Scruffy had accidentally fallen asleep while she was waiting. Gina had been forced to scratch on her door to wake her.

'There were goings on here earlier,' Mavis said gravely. 'According to the plan, I didn't come out of my shed to look. But I heard John and Sal's voices.'

'What?' yelped Max 2. 'You mean they sneaked out here while they thought we were asleep?'

'Yes. They were doing something in the hen house, I'm sure of it,' said Mavis. 'Most of the time they were whispering, but once John dropped something and Sal said … "Ssh! You'll wake the dogs!".'

'They've never worried about that before!' exclaimed Max 1. 'They come in late, turn on lights – even open the fridge in the middle of the night! They don't care who they wake.'

'Ah, but this time they were doing Speckles' bidding, I've no doubt,' said Barney grimly. 'They didn't want your interference. They were making final preparations for her return. Don't forget. This is full moon night. This is the night she'll come. Quickly – we don't have much time!'

He seized the nozzle of the hose and began padding down to the bottom of the yard, where the hen house lay silent and gleaming under the moon. As planned, the Maxes, Scruffy and Gina formed a

line behind him, hauling the hose as it uncoiled like a thin green snake.

Mavis waited at the tap. Her job was perhaps the most important of all, for it was she who was to turn the tap on, at Barney's signal. For this reason, she kept her back firmly turned on the washing hanging on the clothesline just behind her.

Some long striped pyjama pants were flapping gently in the breeze right beside her head. The ends of the legs looked particularly tender.

Mavis longed to turn her head and take a tiny nibble, but she resisted the impulse. She could not afford to lose concentration now. For all she knew, the pyjamas had been put there especially to tempt her from her duty.

A cloud slid across the moon and an eerie darkness fell.

The other dogs close behind him, Barney reached the door of the hen house.

It was locked.

So! Speckles had suspected she was in danger, and had instructed John and Sal to bolt the door against them. Well, they had been prepared for that.

Scruffy sprang into action, digging as she had

never dug before, tunnelling furiously under the hen house wire. Max 1, Max 2 and Gina were right behind her. Barney followed them with the hose.

But it was Scruffy who fearlessly broke through the earth on the other side of the barrier. It was Scruffy who leaped up, shaking herself ... and came face to face with two furious eyes, two flapping wings, and a beak wide open, screeching:

'HOW DARE YOU!'

With a howl of terror, Scruffy fell back, crashing into Gina and the Maxes, who were just emerging from the hole.

Pinned behind them, Barney bellowed, 'Mavis! *Now!*'

The hose came to life. In fact, as the water gushed in a torrent from its nozzle, it seemed to have a life of its own. Hissing, it sprang from Barney's paws and thrashed the ground, its cold, stinging spray arching and flying through the wire into the darkness beyond.

Unearthly shrieks rose from the hen house yard. The air was full of feathers, fur, screeches and cries.

'There are hundreds of them!' screamed Max 1. 'Retreat! Retreat!'

Gasping and stumbling, the dogs pelted back

towards the house. Behind them the hose writhed and water hissed. Lights were going on all around Dolan Street.

'Mavis!' gasped Barney. 'TURN IT OFF!'

And suddenly, there was silence.

'Tomorrow! My place!' Barney muttered. Then he was off.

The other dogs didn't hesitate. In seconds they had streaked away into the darkness, heading for their beds, and safety.

Left alone, Mavis gave the tap a final turn. She wanted to make sure there were no drips. She hated wasting water. Then she, too, trotted back to the fence.

On her way, she took a quick nip of pyjama leg. It tasted as good as it looked.

༄ ༅ ༄

In the morning, after the Pets had left in their cars, the dogs met in Barney's yard.

No one said anything at first. All the friends were still shaken from the events of the night before, and most of them had several painful bruises.

'That hose water was more powerful than I expected,' said Barney at last.

'I turned the tap on well, didn't I?' said Mavis.

Everyone nodded thoughtfully.

'There are twelve hens in the hen house,' said Max 1 in a flat voice. 'They came in that van last night.'

'Ah, yes,' Barney murmured.

'Yes,' said Max 2 coldly. 'We spoke to them earlier. They said they were attacked last night, by a gang of ruffians who sprayed them with icy water, then ran away. We told them we'd make sure it didn't happen again.'

'I am very glad,' sighed Gina, 'that the whole thing happened at midnight, when the birds were asleep.'

No one said anything for a while. Then Barney stirred.

'I see it all now,' he said. 'I only wish I'd known this last night. As it was, I had very little sleep. But if I'd realised that our mission had succeeded –'

'What do you mean, *succeeded*?' snapped Max 1. 'We made complete birds of ourselves! The hen house was only cleaned out because the new hens were coming. It had nothing to do with Speckles, or whatever her name was.'

Barney smiled pityingly.

'There are none so blind as those who will not see,' he sighed. 'Don't you understand, small dog, that if it had not been for us, those hens would have been doomed?'

As the others stared at him, he nodded gravely.

'Doomed,' he repeated. 'Obviously, Speckles had arranged for them to come here.'

Max 1 and Max 2 tried to speak, but Barney gently shook his head and held up a paw for silence.

'Don't you see?' he said. 'Speckles was going to take those hens' bodies for herself. Live on, through them. With our hose water we saved them, and destroyed her evil spirit. Forever.'

'You've got an answer for everything, haven't you?' said Max 2 bitterly.

Barney settled his nose on his paws. 'I wouldn't say that,' he said, yawning. 'But one thing I do know. The hen house is no longer haunted. Dolan Street is safe. And Old Buster would have been proud of us.'

'That's three things,' said Mavis.

But Barney was already asleep.

10 Blackmail

The dogs were very tired after their night's adventure at the hen house. The sun was warm, and the newly cut grass was soft. They were having a pleasant doze when suddenly they were woken in a very unexpected way.

'So there you are,' said a squawky voice.

The dogs looked around, startled. There, staring at them, was a scrawny white hen with a floppy red topknot that hung down over one eye.

'Good morning!' she said brightly. 'I'm Peck. Peck by name, and peck by nature. Get it?'

'How did you get out of the hen house?' snapped Max 1.

Peck shrugged. 'Locks? Easy-peasy!' she cackled. 'Now, look. Let's get down to business. I haven't got all day. You know how it is – grubs to catch, eggs to lay.'

'What – do – you – want?' growled Barney.

The hen's eyes narrowed.

'I know it was you lot who attacked us last night,' she said. 'You may have fooled those other chickens, but you haven't fooled me.'

All the dogs stared, not knowing what to say. Barney was the first to recover.

'Gristle!' he growled, his chest swelling. 'How dare you accuse us of –'

'Of ruthlessly attacking a poor, helpless group of hens?' Peck interrupted. 'I accuse you for the very good reason that you're guilty! Guilty as sin! And I've got proof!'

From under her scrawny wing she took a folded cabbage leaf. Her beady eyes hard as stones, she unwrapped the leaf and showed what was hidden inside it. Two tufts of Scruffy's fur, Max 1's name tag, a burr that exactly matched the burrs on Barney's coat, one of the little metal stars from Gina's collar, and several pieces of straw that could only belong to Mavis.

'I found all these in the mud beside the hen house,' Peck said, tapping her foot. 'Except' – she turned to Mavis – 'except for the straw, *which was beside the tap*! Now, what do you say to that?'

'Say nothing, Mavis,' growled Barney.

'Nothing,' said Mavis obligingly.

Peck threw back her head and gave an unpleasant laugh.

'This proof is enough to send you all to prison,' she cackled, shaking the cabbage leaf in front of their noses. 'Chicken killers! That's what you are.'

'We aren't chicken killers yet,' snarled Max 2. 'But that could change any time, Peck!'

Peck cackled again. 'Don't you threaten me!' she said. 'The chickens back at the house know where I am. And there are at least ten birds watching us from the trees.'

She drew herself up and poked her beak at them rudely.

'I've heard about you lot!' she said. 'You're losing your grip. You're starving. Eating worms. Acting crazy. Selling your beds to keep body and soul together.'

'That – is – a load of – *garbage*!'
Barney looked as if he might
explode.

Peck shrugged. 'What do I
care?' she said. 'The point is,
your names are mud in this
town already. There won't
be any trouble making
another story stick.'

'Are you *threatening* us?'
snarled Barney, bristling all over as the other dogs
exclaimed in shock and anger. 'You'd better be very,
very careful. You puny, scrawny, pin-headed …
chook!'

Peck laughed in his face.

'I'm not scared of you!' she sneered. 'You touch a
feather on my head, dog, and you'll be branded
savage for life. If you live that long.'

The friends fell silent. They all knew that the raid
on the hen house had been innocent. They all knew
they hadn't meant the chickens any harm. But who
would believe them?

Who would ever believe that they'd been trying to
cleanse the place of an evil spirit? Certainly this
spiteful, scrawny hen wouldn't.

Peck watched them with satisfaction.

'So – we understand one another,' she said, tucking the cabbage leaf under her wing again. 'Good. Now. I'm not an unreasonable chicken. I'm willing to forget all about this nasty little incident – for a price.'

'A price?' snapped Max 1.

'What price?' quavered Gina.

Peck tossed her topknot out of her eyes. 'I haven't decided yet,' she said. 'I'll let you know.'

'Blackmail!' growled Barney.

Peck smiled. 'Call it what you like,' she said. 'For now – just think about it.'

With that, she turned and stalked away, her skinny body wobbling on her stick-like legs as she strutted through the hole in the fence and disappeared from sight.

The dogs looked at one another. Mavis saw a pair

of gloves lying in the flower garden, chose one and began to chew it absent-mindedly.

'What are we going to do?' moaned Scruffy.

Max 2 bared his teeth.

'There'll be no spying birds around tonight,' he snarled. 'We'll creep down to the hen house, lure that Peck thing outside, and –'

'Oh, no!' cried Gina in fright.

'Don't worry,' said Max 1. 'He's all yap. He faints at the sight of blood, unless it's on TV.'

'I do not!' Max 2 yelled furiously.

'You do!'

'I'll show you!!'

The Maxes threw themselves at one another and started wrestling, growling ferociously.

Gina wailed in despair.

'Stop it!' roared Barney. 'Whatever you do in your own house, there'll be no fighting in my yard. The birds are all watching, too! Have you no shame?'

The Maxes didn't, it seemed. Locked together, they rolled over and over on the grass.

'If there's one thing I hate, it's violence,' said Mavis distastefully.

She put down the glove, stepped daintily up to the growling bundle of brown fur, lowered her horns, and flicked upwards.

The Maxes sailed up into the air, travelled a short distance, then fell to earth with a thump.

They lay side by side, blinking at the sky. They didn't seem to feel like fighting any more.

'That's better,' said Barney with satisfaction. 'Thank you, Mavis.'

'You're very welcome,' said Mavis, and picked up the glove again.

The Maxes mumbled in a dazed sort of way. The birds in the trees chattered to one another excitedly, then scattered to spread the news that the Dolan Street dogs were trying to learn to fly, and failing miserably.

'Of course we're all upset,' said Gina, trying to be sensible. 'But maybe we're worried about nothing. Maybe Peck was just teasing us.'

'Maybe by tomorrow she'll have forgotten about the whole thing,' added Scruffy hopefully.

Barney frowned and shook his head.

'I don't think so,' he muttered. 'As Old Buster, rest his bones, used to say, a cross hen is a bad enemy.

Hens' brains are very, very small, you know. They can only fit in one thought at a time. And when that thought is revenge …'

He sighed deeply. 'I'm afraid we haven't heard the last of this, my friends. Not by a long way.'

And of course he was right.

$\sim$3$\sim$3$\sim$

No one saw Peck for the rest of that day, and when the friends met again the next morning there was still no sign of her.

Scruffy and Gina had started hoping that, after all, Peck had decided to leave them in peace.

Max 1 and Max 2 were showing signs of boasting that their threats had paid off.

Mavis had helped herself to the second glove from the flower garden. As she said, it looked lonely all by itself, and it would be kindest to put it out of its misery.

Barney, however, was quiet and watchful. For the first time in his life, he had not listened to the morning news, but had stayed inside until it was over.

Scruffy was glad, for his sake. It had been just as bad as the news the day before. Someone had started an appeal for what she called 'our unfortunate friends in Dolan Street'. Garbage Guts had put out a press release claiming that he was planning another escape, so the Dolan Street dogs had better watch out.

The friends were about to go inside to watch 'Dog Hospital' when they heard the slapping of many flat feet coming down the road. They ran to the fence and saw that the approaching visitors were the ducks from the park at the top of the hill.

The ducks were waddling along in a group, looking right and left with interest. When they reached the Maxes' house, they stopped and began flying over the fence.

'Hey, you!' shouted Max 1 and Max 2, pelting back into their own yard with the other dogs following. 'You ducks! What do you think you're doing?'

The head duck stretched his green neck and peered at them haughtily.

'Greetings, dogs,' he said. 'How are the flying lessons going?'

The ducks behind him laughed loudly. Max 1 and Max 2 glared.

'We hear that a small group of hens has settled here,' said the head duck, smoothing the feathers on his already gleaming chest. 'We have come to call on them, to welcome them to the neighbourhood.'

'This is *our* house,' snapped Max 1.

The head duck looked around disdainfully.

'Possibly it is,' he said. 'It looks small and untidy enough to be yours, certainly. But as *we* never prevent *you* from entering *our* park, or paddling your disgustingly furry feet in *our* pond, we presume that you will have no objection to a short visit.'

The Maxes glowered. There was nothing they could say to this.

'Where are the new residents?' demanded the head duck.

'Around the back,' Max 1 muttered sullenly.

With a nod, the head duck turned and led his companions around the side of the house, towards the back yard and the hen house.

The dogs sat and watched them go.

'Who do they think they are?' grumbled Max 2. 'Why should *they* come and welcome the hens?'

'Well, they *are* relations, in a way, Max,' said Gina.

Max 2 stared at her. 'Hens and ducks related?' he jeered. 'That's the stupidest thing I've ever heard. Next, you'll be saying that hens are related to birds!'

'Hens *are* birds!' said Gina crossly.

Max 1 snorted with disbelieving laughter.

'Do hens fly?' he demanded. 'Do hens sit on Mavis's head?'

'That is completely beside the point,' growled Barney. 'You're just showing your ignorance, young dog. All birds have feathers. Ducks and hens have feathers. So ducks and hens are birds. That's all there is to it.'

'Gristle!' said Max 2 rudely. 'All rats have hair. Dogs have hair. Does that mean dogs are rats?'

Barney hesitated.

Mavis swallowed the last finger of the glove.

'"Dog Hospital" is due to start,' she said. 'Are we going to watch it, or not? It's all the same to me.'

11 Revenge Is Sweet

Unfortunately, the 'Dog Hospital' episode that day was about a Chihuahua who had been savagely attacked by two geese. This made Gina rather nervous about birds in general, and also started another long argument between Barney and the Maxes about whether the Chihuahua was a rat or not.

Scruffy had once met a pair of Chihuahuas at the vet's surgery, and knew for a fact that although Chihuahuas were small, they were certainly dogs. But nothing she could say convinced the Maxes – or, at least, so they pretended.

After a while she became certain that they were only keeping up the argument to annoy Barney, so she became quite annoyed herself. And so did Mavis, because the argument kept her awake.

All in all, everyone was feeling quite crabby by the time 'Dog Hospital' ended.

They went back outside and saw that the ducks had finished their visit and were already walking back up the hill towards the park.

'Good riddance,' growled Max 1.

'Uh-oh,' said his brother, pointing. 'Look who's coming.'

It was Peck. She came hurrying through the fence, her topknot flapping wildly, her little eyes flashing with determination.

'I've decided what I want, doggies,' she announced.

'Watch your cheeky tongue!' snarled Barney.

'Don't you forget what I know, Whiskers,' retorted Peck. 'So far I've kept it to myself, but that won't necessarily last. You'd better be polite to me, or you'll be sorry.'

'Why don't you just tell us what you want, Peck?' asked Gina. Even she was controlling her temper with difficulty.

Peck saw that it was time to come to the point.

'We've been chatting to some stuck-up ducks,' she said. 'They've got something we haven't got. And why should they, may I ask? What's so special about them? I want you to make us a pond.'

'Don't be ridiculous!' snorted Barney. 'Hens don't swim.'

Peck seemed to swell up to twice her normal size.

'And why not?' she shrieked, almost spitting with rage. 'Why *shouldn't* hens swim, if they want to?'

'But –' Gina began.

'Shut your beak!' screeched Peck. 'Do you think we're going to be told what we can and can't do by a pack of loser dogs? We want a pond. And we want it now! Or –'

'All right, all right,' said Barney hurriedly.

Peck nodded sharply and turned to lead the way back to the Maxes' house.

'Wait a minute,' snapped Max 1.

Peck swung around, her topknot flopping over one eye.

'What?' she squawked rudely.

'If we agree to do this for you, how do we know you'll keep your side of the deal?' growled Max 1.

'That's right,' Max 2 agreed. 'How do we know you won't keep asking for more, and more, and more?'

Peck scratched the ground furiously.

'Okay, okay, I'll swear!' she said at last. 'I swear that if you dig us a pond, I'll never tell that you attacked the hen house. If I do tell, may my feathers turn to dust. And may the next grub I eat stick in my throat and choke me to death!'

'That seems fair,' said Barney. He turned to the other dogs. 'Are you happy with that?' he asked.

'It's horrible!' said Gina, shuddering.

'As oaths go, it's not too bad,' said Mavis.

Max 1 and Max 2 nodded grudgingly.

Scruffy couldn't say or do anything. She was imagining how it would feel to have a grub stuck in her throat, and the idea made her feel too sick to move.

'Let's go, then,' screeched Peck. 'I've promised the others a pond by sunset, and I want to keep my word. There's no time to waste!'

⋈ ⋈ ⋈

Luckily, the Maxes' Pets had recently removed a large patch of grass near the hen house, to make a vegetable garden. They had dug the soil of the bare patch until it was quite soft and crumbly, but there were no vegetables planted yet.

Everyone agreed that this was an ideal place to dig the pond. For one thing, digging in the bare patch would be much easier and quicker than digging grass. And for another, the Maxes said that they could far more easily do without vegetables than do without the grassy areas of the yard, which were useful for ball games.

The next few hours were very hard work for all the dogs. Except, perhaps, for Mavis, who claimed that digging was bad for her back, and Barney, who bruised his toe in the early stages and had to retire hurt to direct operations.

The others were soon covered in dirt, and very tired. They were also very aware of the birds watching with interest.

Their tempers were not improved by Peck, who stood at the edge of the hole, screeching, 'Faster! Faster!' every time they stopped to rest.

When finally the hole was large and deep enough

to satisfy even Peck, Mavis turned on the hose and they filled it to the brim. The water was muddy, but still gleamed invitingly in the afternoon sun.

'Now *that's* what I call a pond!' said Peck, as the dogs collapsed beside their work.

'Give us back those things you've got under your wing,' mumbled Max 1.

Peck passed over the cabbage leaf impatiently, then puffed up her chest.

'Pond's ready!' she shrieked. 'Come and get it!'

The other hens came rushing from the hen house. They clustered, clucking, around Peck, praising and thanking her, saying, 'You're so clever, Peck!', 'How wonderful!', 'A pond of our very own!', and many other boring, irritating things of the same sort.

Then there was a short silence.

'What do we do now?' asked a short, stubby hen called Daisy.

'Do?' exclaimed Peck. 'Why, we go for a swim, of course!'

Beckoning with one scrawny wing, she rushed to the edge of the pond. The other hens ran after her, squealing with excitement.

Daisy put her foot in the water, then drew it back quickly.

'It's wet!' she squawked.

'Of course it's wet, you stupid hen!' shouted
Max 2. 'It's full of water!'

'Just because it's full of water, that's no reason why
it should be wet!' squawked Daisy's friend, Lilibet.

Daisy nodded her head violently, and so did all
the others.

Peck had begun to look a little stressed.

'Now,' she said, holding up her wings for silence.
'You remember we all decided that it was unfair for
the ducks to have a pond, when we didn't?'

The hens nodded. 'Unfair!', 'Scandalous!', 'Cruel!'
they cackled.

'All right then,' said Peck. 'So I've got us a pond of
our very own.'

'But it's no good!' exclaimed Daisy. 'It's wet!'

'All ponds are wet,' said Peck desperately.

'I'm starting to feel sorry for her,' Gina whispered to Scruffy.

'Don't you dare!' snarled Max 1 and Max 2 together.

Peck cleared her throat and tossed back her topknot.

'We have our own pond,' she said firmly. 'So we will now go for a swim. Follow me!'

She plunged into the water.

The other hens lifted their feet up in disgust as the water lapped at their claws. Then they all turned around and wandered back to the hen house, cackling to one another.

'Peck always was peculiar,' Scruffy heard one of them say.

'What a waste of good dust, wetting it like that,' said another.

'I'm bored,' said Daisy. 'Tell you what, last one to lay an egg has to climb on the roof.'

'Good idea,' the others chorused enthusiastically, breaking into a run.

Peck fluttered on the water's surface for a moment, then sank like a stone. She came up, gasping, then sank again.

'She's drowning!' cried Gina in horror.

'Good,' muttered Max 2.

But already Gina had plunged into the pond. A lot

of the water had already soaked into the dirt, so it didn't take long before she found Peck. In seconds she had hauled the limp body to safety.

Peck's eyelids were fluttering and she was mumbling and moaning. She was soaked through, shivering, and caked with mud.

'So,' said Max 1, strolling to her side. 'Did you have a good swim?'

'Go away,' wailed Peck.

'Don't forget – you swore!' said Max 1, poking the wet feathers.

'Leave her alone,' whispered Scruffy. 'I'm sure she'll remember.'

'I will!' said Peck bitterly. 'I'll remember this as long as I live!'

She turned her skinny neck to glare at the other hens, who were shrieking and flapping towards the hen house roof.

'After all I've done for them,' she squawked. 'How *could* they be so ungrateful? They don't *deserve* a pond!'

She coughed, and spat out some water. 'Fill it in again!' she spluttered.

'*What?*' growled Barney furiously.

'Fill the pond in, I tell you!' screeched Peck. She seemed to be becoming hysterical.

'Let's do it,' said Max 1. 'Then John and Sal can still grow their vegetables. They'd like that.'

So they filled the muddy hole with dirt again – or, at least, the Maxes, Gina and Scruffy did. Mavis had dozed off while Peck was drowning, and Barney still had a sore toe.

Filling the hole didn't take nearly as long as digging it had done, and quite soon the Maxes' yard looked the same as it had before, though a little damper.

The dogs washed their paws under the tap, woke Mavis, and left Peck brooding by the muddy patch of earth that had once been her pond.

'So!' said Barney, leading the way briskly back to the front of the house. 'That's the end of that, I'm glad to say.'

'Being blackmailed is extremely exhausting, though,' sighed Gina, as she limped along behind him. 'I'm aching from head to paw.'

'Me too,' chorused Max 1, Max 2 and Scruffy.

Barney snorted. 'You young dogs haven't got any stamina,' he said. 'Isn't that right, Mavis?'

'I feel fine myself,' said Mavis.

Perhaps it was a sign of just how tired the others were that no one uttered a word of protest. For once, even the Maxes were content to keep their mouths firmly closed. They knew that the sooner they reached their beds, the sooner they could sleep, and they wanted to waste no time on arguments.

It had been a very long day.

12 Rumours

The annoying and embarrassing rumours that the Dolan Street birds had started were still flying around the neighbourhood. Like all rumours, they were very hard to stop.

Garbage Guts and the Danger Corner Rottweilers took great pleasure in spreading them, and adding to them, too. They were the ringleaders, but there were plenty of other bird-brained dogs only too glad to join in.

The Dolan Street dogs had denied the stories, of course, and their close friends believed them, but there were many others who loved to listen to juicy gossip, whether it was true or not.

Almost every day there would be some sly comment on the news about Dolan Street flying lessons, insect-eating or sausage worms.

The story of Scruffy's couch being sold was brought up again quite often. The old one about Mavis being mad kept being repeated. And now, of course, there was the new tale about the dogs digging a pond for the hens, then filling it up again.

To make matters even worse, Garbage Guts was still boasting that he could steal food from Dolan Street whenever he wanted to, and that no one down there could do a thing about it.

It was most frustrating.

Barney was taking it very hard. He said that it was a terrible thing to lose respect at his time of life. He said that Old Buster would turn in his grave if he knew.

'All the dogs who matter know the truth, Barney,' said Gina, trying to comfort him. 'We mustn't take any notice of those others. They'll forget all about it as soon as something else happens to take their minds off us.'

'No,' Barney growled. 'You heard what that Peck creature said. Our name is mud around here, and as Old Buster told me time and again, mud sticks. "Young dog," he'd say to me, "a good reputation is

like a precious bone. It has to be guarded at all costs."
Ah well, it's too late for that now.'

He groaned dismally and glanced under his eyebrows at the Maxes. He seemed, rather unfairly,
Scruffy thought, to blame them for the whole affair.

'It's not our fault!' snapped Max 2. 'It's because
we live down at the bottom of this rotten hill, all
alone, where no one else can see us.'

'That's right,' Max 1 said loudly. 'No wonder weird
rumours spread about us. If we lived up near the
park, in plain sight –'

'Go and live up there then!' snarled Barney,
jumping up in a rage. 'Go and rub shoulders with a
bunch of gossiping, car-chasing bird-brains if you
want! This place is good enough for me.'

'Me, too,' said Mavis. She snatched at a dandelion
and chewed it defiantly.

'Don't fight,' pleaded Gina.

But the Maxes just curled their lips and muttered
to one another, and Barney stalked off into the house
without looking back.

No sooner had he gone than a truck came
rumbling down the street. It lumbered past the
house, stopped, and started to turn around.

'Barney! Truck!' Scruffy shouted urgently.

His eyes wild, Barney came bounding back. He

managed to throw himself down on the ground just as the truck finished its turn and began shuddering away up the hill.

'Look at him! *He's* a fine one to talk about birdbrains,' Max 1 jeered under his breath.

'Muzzle up!' Gina hissed.

When the truck had gone, Barney got up stiffly, shook himself three times, and, without a word to anyone, plodded off to check his food bowl.

He walked slowly, his shoulders slumped, pretending to ignore the birds that were teasing and waving worms above his head. Obviously he had little hope that there would be a sausage waiting for him today, and in her heart Scruffy knew he was right.

Barney had explained many times that Spells had to be followed exactly. Almost certainly, an important part of the Sausage Appearing Spell was that he was lying on his grass when a truck came down the hill.

Today, because of his fight with the Maxes, he had not been in his usual place when the truck arrived. By a terrible stroke of luck, he had missed his chance.

Everything's going wrong, Scruffy thought miserably. She felt terrible. Even the memory of her new couch couldn't cheer her up.

Sure enough, Barney didn't come back, and after a few moments they heard the rattle of his door. He had gone back to bed.

'Poor Barney,' Gina whispered to Scruffy. 'He really isn't himself. If only we could do something about these rumours. Stop the birds and those awful Rottweilers from making us a laughing stock.'

'And Garbage Guts,' said Mavis, overhearing. 'Vulgar thing!' She burped delicately, and reached for another dandelion.

'Let's talk to Tiger, Sunny, Mattie and Deakin about it when we see them on our walk today,' said Scruffy. 'Maybe they can suggest something.'

'We'll come with you. I'd like to see Tiger myself,' Max 1 broke in, smiling wickedly. 'He's got a new coat, I hear.'

'They say it's got a bow at the back,' sniggered Max 2. 'And a little hood with fancy ear holes.'

'Oh, I'm sure that's not true,' said Gina. But she smiled anyway.

'It is!' Max 1 insisted. 'It was on the news. It *must* be true!'

Scruffy sighed, but didn't say anything. What was the point?

☙❧☙

By that evening, a nasty wind had begun to blow, and it took Scruffy quite a while to persuade Zac to let her take him for a walk. It was Zac's turn for exercise, but he tended to be a bit lazy, especially in bad weather.

At last, however, Scruffy managed to make him see reason. She collected her lead while Zac put on a coat, then they set off. Zac was sulking and dragging his feet, but she pretended not to notice.

Gina and Caroline were walking slowly up the hill in front of them. Scruffy helped Zac to hurry, and they soon caught up.

Zac and Caroline began gabbling together, nodding their heads and moving their hands around as Pets always did when they met. Good, thought Scruffy. That ought to cheer Zac up.

Some dogs – Deakin the Boxer, for example – didn't believe that Pets talked sense to one another. But all the Dolan Street dogs knew that this wasn't true. Sure, Pets didn't make sounds that dogs thought of as words. But they could still communicate, in a simple way.

'Where are the Maxes?' Scruffy whispered to Gina.

'Maybe they're not coming,' Gina whispered back. 'I wouldn't really mind if they didn't, would you? If they tease Tiger about his new coat, he'll get crabby, and won't be any help to us at all.'

They reached the top of the hill. The park was just ahead of them, but they turned away from it and gently guided Caroline and Zac to the left.

Lately, they had been avoiding the park. Walking there was no longer pleasant. The ducks had taken to calling out sarcastic remarks, and dogs they hardly knew stared and whispered as they passed.

They had asked Mattie, Sunny, Deakin and Tiger to meet them instead at The Place of Good Smells.

'I hope they'll be able to help us,' said Scruffy.

'Yes,' Gina answered. 'I can't take much more of this.'

She looked around at the car-lined street, at the pavements, houses and traffic lights.

'I've been thinking, you know,' she went on in a low voice. 'In a way, though I hate to admit it, the Maxes are right. Because we live all the way down at the bottom of Dolan Street, we're cut off from everyday life up here. Most of the neighbourhood dogs only see us now and then. They don't know much about us.'

Scruffy thought about that. 'You mean – to them we seem sort of mysterious?' she asked.

Gina nodded. 'That's right. So of course we're interesting to gossip about. It's only natural. And it's so easy for dogs to get the wrong idea about us.'

'Well, we'll just have to think of a way of giving them the *right* idea, for a change,' said Scruffy.

Gina glanced at her with admiration. 'You're such a positive thinker, Scruffy,' she said warmly.

Scruffy twitched her ears with embarrassed pleasure, and trotted on briskly. But after a moment she slowed down again.

She wished she felt as confident as she had sounded.

13 The Place of Good Smells

The Place of Good Smells was at the end of a narrow track just past the park. It was a small, pretty hollow, where a little bridge crossed a muddy patch choked with reeds.

Pets sometimes dumped rubbish in the muddy patch, and over the years the Place had developed a whole range of particularly interesting scents.

It had another big advantage as a meeting place. Tiger lived right next door.

Tiger's old Pet, Grace, always worked in the garden till it was too dark to see. She was a small, brown, wrinkled Pet with white hair fluffing out around her ears and a very friendly smile. Like most Pets, she loved company. She could be relied upon to call over the fence to any other Pet she saw walking in The Place of Good Smells.

This was very handy. Knowing that their Pets were safe and happily occupied with Grace, dogs were free to chat without feeling they were neglecting their responsibilities.

Tiger, Sunny, Mattie and Deakin were waiting by the bridge, enjoying the fragrance of the air and remarking on the various new smells they had noticed. Mattie, Sunny and Deakin's Pets were already in Tiger's garden. They were also using their noses for once, smelling flowers with Grace. They all called out to Zac and Caroline, who went to join them.

Scruffy was relieved to see that Tiger's new coat was almost exactly the same as the old one. Very plain, with red checks and just two, quite small, brass buckles.

'Oh, you've got a new coat, Tiger,' said Gina, acting surprised. 'It's very smart.'

'Dinna pretend ye havena heard about it, lassie,' Tiger said gruffly, his Scots accent particularly strong, as it always was when he was cross. 'But as ye can see, that business about the wee hood was a load of gristle!'

'And the bow,' added Sunny, grinning.

Deakin gave a sudden snort of laughter, and turned away hastily, pretending to scratch his back leg.

Tiger's eyes gleamed dangerously. 'It's no laughing matter,' he growled. 'I've had a verra bad day. I had to bite three dogs, no less, before lunch. They were trying to get through the fence to take a look at me. As if I havena got enough to do!'

'Zee news is becoming a disgrace!' Mattie said, shaking her curly black head. 'Zeese days, you cannot believe a single word you 'ear.'

'That's what we wanted to talk to you about,' said Gina. 'We've got to do something about these Dolan

Street rumours. They're really upsetting Barney.'

'Putting him right off his worms, eh?' grinned Deakin. He was only joking, but it seemed to Scruffy that the joke was in bad taste.

At that moment, Max 1 and Max 2 came tearing into The Place of Good Smells, dragging John and Sal behind them.

'Sorry we're late,' shouted Max 1. He jerked his head and expertly freed John from the lead. Max 2 did the same with Sal. Then both dogs pounded towards the bridge, without looking back.

'You shouldn't just take John and Sal off the lead and leave them, you two,' Gina scolded. 'They might wander onto the road.'

'Not them. They're too smart,' said Max 2 carelessly. 'They'll go over to see Grace. They like her.'

Sure enough, John and Sal were heading straight for Tiger's fence. Scruffy felt a small pang of anxiety as she saw Zac turning stiffly to greet them. Zac sometimes snapped at John and Sal when they met.

Zac wasn't usually aggressive. It was the Maxes' fault, really. They didn't do a thing to stop Sal and John playing loud music late at night, and Zac liked his sleep.

Many times in the past, Barney had told the Maxes to keep their Pets more under control at night. But the Maxes said that as long as they were having a good time, they didn't see why John and Sal couldn't have a good time as well. They said that Barney couldn't talk anyway, because he let Bert and Alice have the TV on as loudly as they liked.

Barney had no choice, of course, because Bert and Alice were a little deaf, and he, if the truth be known, was becoming a trifle hard of hearing himself. So in the end he stopped talking about noise, and the Maxes went on letting Sal and John do exactly as they liked.

Scruffy didn't want to have to leave the meeting to stop a fight. So she was relieved to see, after a moment, that on this occasion Zac seemed to be behaving well. Perhaps it was because he was in Tiger's garden. Or because Caroline was with him. Like Gina, Caroline liked peace.

Max 2 bounced over to Tiger, and examined the new coat.

'Nice and warm, is it, Tige?' he enquired cheekily.

'Aye,' said Tiger. And something about the way he said it made Max 2 quieten down quite quickly.

'About the rumours,' said Gina, determined to keep on the subject. 'What can we do to stop them?'

'Not a thing, in my opinion,' said Tiger. 'Just bite anyone who looks at ye sideways. That's what I do.'

'I don't think biting's really my sort of thing,' Gina said doubtfully.

Tiger shrugged. 'I canna help those who will na help themselves,' he grunted.

'I heard a crazy story this morning. About you digging a pond for hens,' chortled Sunny. 'How stupid would a dog have to be to do a thing like that?'

Gina, Scruffy and the Maxes glanced at one another, but said nothing.

'I myself have done everysing I can to stop zee talk,' said Mattie. 'I tell everyone I meet – zeese stories of Dolan Street are not true! But zey do not believe me. Imbeciles!'

'You've got to face it – dogs love to talk,' said Deakin. 'The crazier the stories are, the more they like 'em. It's just a bit of fun.'

'Not fun when it's happening to you,' said Max 2 sourly. 'And stuck down in Dolan Street, what can we do about it?'

The wind was rising, whipping the curls on Mattie's ears into knots. She smoothed them with an elegant paw.

'Sunny and I 'ave given zis much thought,' she said. 'Perhaps zee way to fight zeese rumours is to begin anozzer

141

rumour altogezzer. One zat brings credit to you, instead of making you look foolish, *non*?'

Again, Gina, Scruffy and the Maxes glanced at one another.

'You know, that's not a bad idea,' said Max 1 slowly. 'Another rumour. But a good one. A really good one. One that makes us out to be heroes.'

'Yes!' Scruffy's heart was beating fast.

Only Gina was looking doubtful.

'It wouldn't be right to tell a lie,' she murmured.

'Oh, don't be such a Goody-Four-Paws,' snapped Max 2. 'It's all in a good cause.'

'Self-defence!' said Sunny.

'Just a bit of fun,' urged Deakin. 'No harm in it.'

'It would be better, certainly, if you could say somesing zat was true,' said Mattie. 'Yet, if zere is nozzing good to say …?' She paused delicately.

'But we *do* have –' Scruffy began.

'Scruffy!' Gina broke in warningly, and Scruffy broke off, biting her lip.

Of course, Gina was right. However much they wanted to, they couldn't tell about saving the world. They had promised to keep the secret.

Scruffy could see from the Maxes' faces that they were thinking the same thing. Max 2's face was twisted into a quite frightening snarl of frustration.

'What's up with you?' demanded Deakin, staring.

'Nothing,' scowled Max 1, nudging his brother viciously.

Mattie and Sunny waited. They were far too well mannered to ask questions.

'It's a good idea,' said Gina at last. 'We'll think about it.'

'Don't fret,' grinned Deakin. 'Something's bound to turn up.'

'Mebbe,' said Tiger darkly. 'But if ye take my advice, ye'll forget this namby-pamby rubbish, sharpen up your teeth, and use them. A dog has to do what a dog has to do.'

Scruffy heard Gina sigh, and felt rather like sighing herself. Her high hopes had started to die down.

Mattie and Sunny's idea had sounded good at first, but Scruffy feared it wouldn't work after all.

It was all right for Garbage Guts to boast about things that hadn't happened, and tell everyone how wonderful and clever he was. The Maxes could probably do it just as well.

But Barney would never agree to such a thing. He had far too much pride. And Gina had never boasted in her life.

No, thought Scruffy. It's like Deakin says. We'll just have to hope something turns up.

14 The Night the Burglars Came

That night, just before bedtime, while Scruffy took a final walk in the garden and listened to the wild wind, the Maxes ate a late-night snack and argued about what would be the most flattering rumour they could spread about themselves.

At the same moment, Mavis, alone in her shed with only straw to eat, was wishing that Scruffy had brought a leafy twig back from her walk, and thinking about tree varieties.

And Barney, lying on his blanket, was mourning his lost reputation and planning revenge on Garbage Guts.

Meanwhile, in Gina's house, an event was

occurring that would change everything. In other words, something was turning up.

The phone rang. Caroline answered it, and at once Gina knew that something was wrong.

Caroline exclaimed in the way she did if she accidentally trod on Gina's foot. She gasped the name of her friend, Suzanne, several times. Then she gabbled for a few moments more, hung up, and ran into the room where her bed was.

Gina followed, and saw Caroline throwing some clothes into a bag. It was one of the bags Caroline always used when they went to stay at Bluey's farm, at Christmas.

Caroline ran into the bathroom and came back with the little brush she had to use to clean her teeth, because she hardly ever chewed bones.

This was the final proof. They were going away somewhere.

It must have something to do with that phone call, Gina thought.

She ran and got her lead. Caroline was in such a state that it was possible she'd forget to pack it.

But when Caroline saw the lead she didn't make a move to take it. She just dropped to her knees beside Gina and started trying to talk to her, stammering out some of the few words of Dog she knew, like, 'No, Gina' – 'Good   girl' – 'Stay' – 'Suzanne' – 'Cats' – 'Home' – 'Breakfast'.

Then she gave Gina a hug, stood up, and ran to the kitchen cupboard. She took out a dog biscuit and put it in Gina's bowl.

Surprised, but relieved that at last Caroline seemed to be calming down, Gina began eating the biscuit. It took her full attention for quite a few minutes, but when she had swallowed the last crumb, she realised that the house was suspiciously silent.

She went back to the living room and saw to her horror that the main light had been turned off. Then she heard the sound of the car engine outside.

Caroline had crept out the front door without her knowing. Caroline was running away!

Gina ran to her own door in the kitchen, scrambled through it and hurried outside.

But she was too late. By the time she got to the

front of the house, the driveway gates were shut and
Caroline was driving away into the night.

Shocked, Gina sat down on the cold grass, trying
to work out what had happened. Quite often, on
'Dog Hospital', Pets answered the phone, listened for
a moment, gabbled something, and then ran out of
the house to their cars, exactly as Caroline had done.

It usually meant that someone had been injured
and needed help. Caroline had been speaking to
Suzanne. Perhaps …

Scruffy came running to the gap in the fence and
poked her nose through.

'I saw Caroline leaving!' she gasped, raising her
voice so that Gina could hear her above the wind. 'She
had a bag with her. Don't tell me she's going away?'

'Yes,' Gina said slowly. She'd at last worked out what Caroline had been trying to tell her.

'Her friend Suzanne is in some sort of trouble,' she told Scruffy. 'Caroline's going to help. I can't go with her, because there are three horrible cats in that house, and I wouldn't get a wink of sleep. She'll be home in time for breakfast.'

'You mean you'll be in the house alone all *night*?' Scruffy shook her head in disbelief. 'How could Caroline *do* such a thing?'

'It was an emergency,' Gina said loyally. She wouldn't hear a word against Caroline.

She said goodnight to Scruffy and walked back to the house as if she didn't have a care in the world. But in her heart she quivered at the thought of the long, dark, lonely night ahead.

Burglars came in the night. Gina knew that from watching television with Caroline in the evenings. The idea made her quite nervous, but she had always felt safe when she went to bed, because she knew that Caroline would protect her if a burglar came.

Tonight is going to be different, Gina thought, as she crept into the kitchen. The light was still on there, at least. That was one thing to be thankful for.

Her claws scrabbled loudly on the shiny floor. Everything was very still and clean. As usual, Gina

and Caroline had tidied the kitchen together after dinner. They always shared the work fairly. Gina ate the scraps and cleaned up any crumbs from the floor, and Caroline washed the dishes.

Just thinking about that made Gina feel lonely.

Without Caroline, the house seemed very empty. Wind howled outside, and the windows rattled.

Gina went through to the dim living room, jumped onto the couch and curled herself up into the smallest ball she could.

No doubt burglars far and wide were already hearing the news that there was only an unprotected dog in the pink house at the bottom of Dolan Street. In an hour or two they would all be putting on their masks and gloves and creeping down the hill.

Gina's mouth felt dry. I must pull myself together, she thought. I'm not a pup. Caroline believes in me. She thinks I can cope, or she'd never have left me to face the burglars alone.

That thought gave her courage.

I must make a plan, she thought. For when they come.

The first thing, surely, was to hide all the valuables in the house. The second was to find a place to hide herself.

Gina got down from the couch, and set to work.

Her lead, her food bowl and her brush were fairly easy to hide under the couch cushions. The water bowl was more difficult, because it was very full. The best she could do was to drag it under the coffee table. With a bit of luck, she thought, the trail of water that had spilled on the way would have soaked into the carpet by the time the burglars arrived, and they wouldn't notice it.

Luckily, Caroline had been in such a hurry that she hadn't closed the food cupboard door properly, so it swung open as soon as Gina pawed at it. She put the dog treats packet under the cushions with her lead and other things, then went back for the dog biscuits.

The bag of biscuits was so large that it took all her energy to drag it into the living room and hide it behind the curtains. A few biscuits fell out on the way, so she ate them. She knew she had to keep up her strength.

After that, there were just a few cans of dog food. They were quite heavy but rolled easily, and were quickly hidden behind the wood basket that stood in front of the fireplace.

Gina was just about exhausted by now, but there was one thing left to do. She had to create her own hiding place.

She took her rug from the corner of the sunroom and dragged it to the couch. It was hard work spreading it out so that it covered the couch completely, but at last Gina was satisfied that it looked quite natural.

Carefully she crawled under the rug and snuggled down till only the tip of her nose was showing. The cushions felt a bit lumpy because of all the things stuffed beneath them, but she knew that couldn't be helped.

She gave a long, low sigh of relief. Now all she had to do when the burglars came was to keep very still and quiet. She, and all the things of real value in the house, were safe.

Her eyes were very heavy. The rug was warm and cosy.

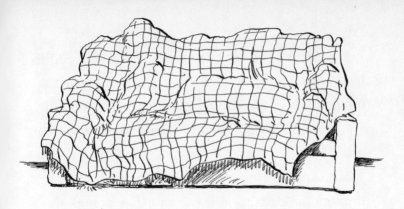

I've done everything I can, she thought. Now I'd better get some sleep.

❧❧❧

Meanwhile, Scruffy was lying awake on her nice firm bed in the laundry. She was very worried. Her Pets and Petlings had gone to bed, but she couldn't sleep. She didn't even feel like moving onto her couch in the family room.

She hated the thought of Gina being all alone in the house next door. She suspected that her friend felt much worse about it than she had admitted. The danger of burglars was something they had often discussed.

I can't leave her to face the burglars by herself, Scruffy thought. I just can't!

She got out of bed and crept outside.

There was no moon, and the wind was moaning through the trees. The bushes thrashed, the houses creaked.

Scruffy fought her way to the hole in the side fence, making sure to move slowly so that the medals on her collar wouldn't jingle and wake Zac and Julie. She knew they would worry if they knew what she was doing.

She slipped through the fence. Light glowed dimly through the curtains at the front of Gina's house.

Scruffy crept around to the back, where Gina's dog door was. She scratched gently at the door and called Gina's name.

There was no answer.

Cautiously, she poked her head into the kitchen.

The light was on. She could see everything very clearly. And what she saw made her blood run cold.

The food cupboard door was hanging open. The packet of dog treats had gone. The dog biscuits, too. And Gina's food and water bowls were nowhere to be seen.

A shiver ran down Scruffy's spine. The burglars must have arrived already! There had been no cars parked outside in the street, or in Gina's driveway. But perhaps burglars didn't drive cars.

Gina was probably tied up and gagged, lying helpless in a corner somewhere, while the burglars loaded their sacks with all her most precious possessions.

Scruffy felt the hair prickling on the back of her neck. Her mind whirled as she tried desperately to think what she could do.

She knew she was too small to tackle a gang of burglars by herself. She needed help.

Barney said he always slept with one eye open, so he could be alert instantly if his house needed defending. And Mavis's horns were sharp enough to make any burglar think twice about fighting her.

Scruffy turned and ran, heading for Barney's house.

15 Heroes

To Scruffy's surprise, Barney took a while to answer his door. In fact, if Scruffy hadn't known better, she would have thought that he had been sleeping very heavily when she knocked.

A tuft of hair was sticking up on the top of Barney's head. His eyes were bleary. The whiskers on one side of his face were strangely bent.

'I'm sorry to wake you,' Scruffy whispered. 'But it's an emergency.'

'Whasit?' mumbled Barney, staring at her as if he'd never seen her before. Then his eyes focused. He shook himself violently and licked his lips.

'Wake me?' he said in a thick voice. 'Don't you worry about that. I always sleep with one eye open. Always on the alert, that's me. What's wrong?'

Words tumbling over one another, Scruffy stuttered out the story about the burglars in Gina's house.

'Gina tied up and gagged, you say?' growled Barney, the hair starting to rise on his back to match the hair on his head. 'All the valuables gone?'

'Yes. The burglars must be packing their sacks right now,' Scruffy panted. 'Soon they'll be making their getaway. We've got to stop them!'

'Well, why didn't you *call* for help, you foolish young dog?' exclaimed Barney, pushing through the door. 'Why waste time coming all the way over here?'

'I thought they might take Gina hostage if I startled them,' said Scruffy. 'Then our paws would be tied. I thought we should creep in and take them by surprise.'

'Hmm. You might be right.' Barney thought for a moment. Then he swung into action.

'You get the Maxes,' he snapped. 'I'll get Mavis. I don't think she'll wake up for anyone but me. We'll all meet in Gina's front yard. But tell the Maxes to be quiet!'

'I will,' Scruffy promised.

She shot away to the front of the house, and hurried through the side fence, her fur blown straight back by the raging wind.

Max 1 and Max 2 were playing cards by the light of the outside lamp that shone through their bedroom window. Max 1 was quite pleased to see Scruffy, because he was losing. Max 2 wasn't so pleased.

'What's up?' whispered Max 1. 'Something exciting?'

Scruffy told them.

'Burglars?' growled Max 2, baring his teeth. 'Let me at them! I'll tear them limb from limb.'

Scruffy looked worried. She didn't think Gina would like blood on her carpet.

'Take no notice of him,' said Max 1, leading the way through the door. 'Winning at cards always makes him aggressive. He'll settle down.'

They sped silently through Barney's place, through the swampy patch at the end of Dolan Street, and into Gina's front yard.

Barney and Mavis arrived not long afterwards. Mavis had straw in her hair, and was rather cross at being woken.

'I was having such a wonderful dream!' she said. 'I was dreaming I could fly. And just as I was swooping into a field *filled* with thistles, and with the most *glorious* tree in the middle, I had to wake up!'

'Burglars are like that,' said Max 2. 'Very inconsiderate. Now, what's the plan?'

'We creep into the house, then rush out all at once and take the burglars by surprise,' said Barney. 'We mustn't make a sound beforehand, otherwise the burglars might take Gina hostage. Then our paws will be tied.'

'Very clever, Barney,' said Mavis approvingly.

Barney shrugged.

'Don't you think Barney's clever?' Mavis said to Scruffy.

Scruffy nodded, but she had a niggling feeling that something was unfair, somewhere.

They all held their breath as they crept through Gina's dog door. Barney was first, Scruffy was second, Max 1 and Max 2 were next, and Mavis was last.

'I can't hear any burglars,' hissed Max 2. 'I can't hear anything! Except the wind.'

'Be quiet!' exclaimed Mavis, who was having trouble getting through the door behind him. 'Do you *want* Gina to be taken hostage?'

'It might be interesting,' said Max 1. 'We've never had a dognapping in Dolan Street before.'

Barney frowned. 'There's a trail of water on the floor,' he whispered. 'That will lead us to them. Come on!'

He lay down and started crawling on his belly, keeping his head low. The others followed. All except Mavis, who was still stuck in the door.

They reached a place that Scruffy recognised as the living room. It was dim and shadowy. The only light came from a lamp in the hallway.

A large object, strangely shaped, stood in front of a coffee table, facing the television set.

'It's only the couch,' breathed Scruffy in Barney's ear. 'But there's something wrong with it. It's covered in a rug. And it's all lumpy.'

'Ambush!' Barney breathed back. 'The burglars are hiding under that rug, waiting to jump out at us. Well, I'll show them!'

'Yeah, you show them, Barney,' said Max 2. 'We'll be right behind you.'

'Quite a long way behind,' muttered Max 1.

Barney took a deep breath.

'CHARGE!' he yelled.

He sprang at the couch. Scruffy sprang with him. And at exactly the same moment, the lump under the rug swelled and thrashed, and a terrified, muffled shrieking began.

'Burglars! Murderers! Help! HELP!!!'

That's Gina's voice! thought Scruffy. In fury she lunged at the rug, grabbing its fringe in her teeth.

'Where's Gina? What have you done with her?' she growled, hauling with all her strength.

The lump inside the rug screamed and heaved, and Scruffy was swung off her feet. She squealed and hung on for dear life.

Meanwhile, Barney had hurled himself onto the lump from the other end of the couch, and was trying to wrestle with it.

'I'll teach you!' he snarled.

With a final yell the lump tumbled off the couch,

rolling itself up in the rug, and taking Barney and Scruffy with it.

The air was suddenly filled with flying objects.

Dog treats scattered. Gina's brush hit a brass vase like a gong. Her lead soared upward, then fell, tangling around Barney's scrabbling feet.

'Snake!' Barney roared. Kicking to free himself from the lead, he threw himself backwards and crashed into the coffee table.

The coffee table toppled over, throwing magazines everywhere and smashing into the wood basket. The wood basket fell over in turn, and sticks spilled out onto the floor, mixing with the dog treats. Cans of dog food rolled everywhere.

Barney fought on, tumbling over and over on the carpet with the fighting, heaving lump in the rug.

Scruffy bumped along beside them, still holding onto the rug's fringe. Battered and bruised as she was, she wasn't going to give up.

Her heart leaped as she saw that the rug was starting to unroll. She made one last, desperate effort, heaved with all her strength …

And Gina, panting and dazed, flopped out onto the carpet.

It was a while before everything was sorted out, and afterwards Gina, in particular, took a long time to calm down. This was understandable. It would upset anyone to think she was being attacked in her sleep by a gang of ferocious burglars.

Barney was also very ruffled. He felt, quite naturally, that he had been made to look foolish. He blamed Scruffy for the whole affair, and Scruffy thought he was probably right, so she felt very ashamed, as well as sore.

Max 1 and Max 2 couldn't be found. In the end, a crunching sound led the others to look behind the curtains.

It seemed that the Maxes had taken refuge there when the screaming began. As they explained, they'd thought it best to keep out of the way so as not to add to the confusion. Meanwhile, they'd found the

bag of dog biscuits, and had
eaten quite a few, to keep up
their strength.

Mavis had managed to
wriggle back out of the
dog door and had
returned to the grass
at the front of the
house. There she
had gone to sleep,
so she had missed
all the excite-
ment. Gina's

screams and Barney's shouts hadn't woken her.

None of the Dolan Street Pets had woken, either.

'It's disgraceful. We could have all been killed!'
fumed Barney. 'We could be lying here, dead, right
now, and they'd never know.'

'The wind was probably too loud for them to hear
anything,' said Gina, gathering her scattered dog
treats before the Maxes could eat them all. 'And it
doesn't really matter anyway, Barney. After all, we
aren't lying here dead, are we?'

'That's not the point!' Barney frowned disapprov-
ingly. 'We *could* have been lying here dead. *That's*
the point. And not a single Pet came to look. That

would never have happened in my day. When I was a pup, Pets knew their duty. Wind or no wind.'

He licked his leg crossly. He had stood in the water bowl when the coffee table was knocked over.

Gina looked around the room.

'What a mess!' she sighed. 'And Caroline isn't here to clean it up.'

'Well, we'll be going now,' said Max 1 and Max 2, beginning to edge away.

'Oh no you don't!' Barney snapped. 'We're in this together. You stay and help, or there's no "Dog Hospital" for you next week.'

So the dogs tidied the living room as best they could. It took a very long time.

The Maxes grumbled at first, but then they started finding stray biscuits and dog treats in unexpected places, so they stopped complaining.

Scruffy worked very hard, to try to make up for the mistake she'd made.

Gina worked hard, too, because in her heart she was very grateful to her friends for coming to save her, even if things hadn't worked out so well.

Barney kept a sharp eye on activities from the couch.

By sunrise, the wind had dropped, the room was looking more the way it usually did, and everyone was feeling much better.

Talking about being dead had made them all realise that it was good to be alive, even if being alive had some problems. And, as Gina said, it was much better *not* to see a burglar than to see one, if you had the choice.

They went outside and found Mavis enjoying an early breakfast in Gina's flower garden. There was a soft breeze, and the sky was clear. In the trees, young birds were twittering, pestering their parents for food.

It was going to be a good day, perfect for sleeping.

Dogs were already shouting in the distance, telling one another the early morning news.

To the friends' surprise, the news was all about how Gina of Dolan Street had been taken hostage by a ferocious gang of burglars in black masks and gloves, and how the other Dolan Street dogs had heroically rescued her.

The Dolan Street dogs, the news went on, had driven off the gang. It had been a gang of at least twenty, someone said, though another dog, who identified herself as Goldie from Dead Tree Place, said *she* had heard it was only twelve.

Barney, Scruffy, Gina and the Maxes looked at one another. Then they all looked at Mavis.

She shrugged, chewing. 'I only told one bird,' she said.

'It only takes one, Mavis,' said Barney severely. 'You know what they're like.'

'There weren't *any* burglars, Mavis,' Gina said. 'It was all a mistake.'

'Oh, really?' Mavis licked a pink petal from her bottom lip. 'Well, how was I to know? I was asleep, wasn't I?'

For a few moments the dogs discussed the question of whether they should try to spread the word that the story of the burglary had been a little exaggerated.

Gina thought they should. Scruffy wasn't sure. Max 1 and Max 2 thought they shouldn't. Mavis said she didn't care. So Barney had the casting vote, and in the end he decided that correcting the story would be too difficult.

'It might be best to leave things as they are, for now,' he said. 'Otherwise, some ill-natured animals might not understand, and might start saying we aren't heroes after all. Which, of course, would be quite wrong.'

Another round of news began, and the friends noted with pleasure that the number of Dolan Street burglars had risen to twenty-five. The phrase 'Dolan Street heroes' was mentioned several times.

'This'll give those loudmouth Rottweilers something to think about, anyhow,' said Barney with satisfaction.

'And that mongrel Garbage Guts,' said Max 2.

'As you say, young dog,' smiled Barney. 'It's not every day that a ferocious gang of burglars gets driven off around these parts. Twenty-five burglars. Just think of it.'

'Twenty, actually,' Mavis corrected him.

'Goldie says there were only twelve,' Max 1 reminded her.

Scruffy looked confused. 'There *weren't* any burglars at *all*,' she murmured.

'But there *could* have been, Scruffy,' Gina said. 'There could have been any number of burglars. And still, *not even knowing how many burglars there were*, you faced them. You saved me.'

She beamed around at them all.

'You're true heroes,' she said warmly. '*That's* the important thing.'

And no one, not even Scruffy, could disagree with that.

16 The Travelling Salesdog

Life changed dramatically for the Dolan Street dogs after The Night the Burglars Came.

Silly Dolan Street stories were no longer the main feature of the news. Now there were dozens of burglar stories. Burglars feared, heard, or even seen, all over the neighbourhood. Burglar gangs reported prowling the park, lurking around the shops and creeping through the streets.

And the story of how the Dolan Street heroes attacked and drove off forty-three armed burglars, and saved their friend Gina from certain death, was repeated again and again.

Gina and Scruffy had told Mattie, Sunny, Tiger

and Deakin the truth about that story. Mattie, Sunny, Tiger and Deakin had decided to say nothing. After all, as Tiger said, no one believed them when they said the *other* stories were wrong. So what was the point of trying to correct this one?

'What's done is done,' he said. 'And it's a good tale. I canna see the point of spoiling it.'

'It would be a *crime* to spoil it,' Sunny agreed. 'Under the circumstances.'

'*Bien!*' Mattie nodded, and shook back her ears.

Deakin grinned and said, 'I told you something'd turn up!'

༄༅༄༅

One sleepy afternoon, not long afterwards, a stranger came strolling down the Dolan Street hill.

The stranger's legs were long. His fur was dusty and shaggy. Around his neck he wore a faded red bandanna, casually tied, and saddlebags hung on either side of his back.

Scruffy, Gina and the Maxes ran to Barney's gate and looked through the wire as the stranger drew near. Mavis wandered after them, looking with interest at the red bandanna.

Barney got up slowly and yawned.

'Don't get yourselves all excited,' he said. 'It's only a travelling salesdog. The roads were crawling with

them when I was a pup, and times were hard. Why, I've seen more travelling salesdogs than you've had brisket bones. Many's the time Old Buster said to me –'

'I've never had a brisket bone in my life,' said Mavis. 'Or seen a travelling salesdog, either. What is it?'

Barney had been dying for her to ask. But just as he took a deep breath, the stranger, who had reached the gate and overheard, answered for him.

'The travelling salesdog, Madame,' he said, bowing to Mavis in a most gentledoggy fashion, 'is the king of the road. The name is Raymond. At your service.'

A king! Mavis, Gina and Scruffy were fascinated. They pressed their noses harder against the gate wire.

Max 1 and Max 2 weren't impressed.

'You don't look like a king to me,' jeered Max 1.

Raymond smiled. 'Wait till you see what I have in my saddlebags, young sir,' he said. 'Then you may change your mind.'

'We don't want to buy any of your rubbish,' Barney growled. 'Be off with you!'

The stranger looked disappointed, then shrugged and sat down with a sigh.

'Ah, well. I'll just rest for a moment before I turn back, if you don't mind,' he said. 'Normally I wouldn't have come all the way down here. But curiosity got the better of me, unfortunately.'

He looked around. 'I heard that there were some hero dogs at the bottom of this hill. Naturally, I was keen to see them. It would be something to tell the old dogs at home. Could you tell me where these magnificent canines are?'

'Oh,' said Mavis, very pleased. 'Hero dogs? Well, that's us, as a matter of fact.'

'That's right!' chorused Max 1 and Max 2.

'Indeed?' Raymond exclaimed, jumping to his feet with a beaming smile. 'Well, this *is* an honour! Ah, this makes my whole long journey worthwhile.'

Barney cleared his throat loudly. 'Thank you,' he said. 'And now, perhaps, we'll say goodbye. As you can understand, being heroes, we are – quite busy.'

Raymond nodded. 'Of course,' he said humbly. 'But I wonder … I've walked very far today. Could I trouble you for a small drink of water, before I go on my way?'

The other dogs turned and looked at Barney.

'There's a duck pond in the park at the top of the hill,' Barney said coldly.

Raymond licked his dry lips.

'Oh, let him come in, Barney,' said Mavis. 'He looks harmless.'

'Please, Barney!' whispered Gina. 'He looks so tired!'

Barney shrugged. 'Oh, all right,' he growled. 'Around the side, through the bushes there,' he said to Raymond, pointing the way through the frogs' swampy ground. 'But just for a drink, mind you. We won't be buying anything.'

'Fine, fine,' said Raymond, and he moved off quite nimbly, for a dog who was exhausted.

In a minute or two he was clambering through the side fence, and into Barney's yard. He looked around admiringly.

'Beautiful place you have here,' he said to Barney.

'It's not bad,' said Barney, pleased in spite of himself.

'Oh, yes,' said Raymond. 'I've seen many, many properties in my time, but this is what I call superior. And did I see a field at the back when I came through? Don't tell me that's yours as well?'

Barney puffed up his chest and lifted his chin.

'As a matter of fact it is,' he said carelessly.

'And mine,' said Mavis, pushing forward.

Raymond heaved a great sigh.

'Magnificent!' he said. 'Well, well. This *will* be something to tell the old dogs back home.'

'He's laying it on a bit thick, isn't he?' muttered Max 2. Gina frowned at him warningly.

'The water bowl is at the side of the house,' said Barney, in a much friendlier tone. 'Help yourself.'

'Thank you, Barney,' said Raymond. 'Hope you don't mind – I couldn't help overhearing your name. Now, Barney's a name I've always liked. Distinguished, I've always thought. It suits you down to the ground, if I may say so.'

Behind Raymond and Barney's backs, Max 2 was pretending to throw up.

His brother nudged him roughly.

'Leave me alone!' Max 2 complained.

'Do you want to see what's in the saddlebags, or not?' Scruffy heard Max 1 whisper. 'Who knows what's in there. Magic tricks, maybe. Masks. Jokes.

There might even be a rubber sausage. Think what we could do with that!'

Max 2's eyes gleamed wickedly, and he went very quiet.

Raymond went to the water bowl and took a short drink. When he had finished, he came back to the others and sat down, shrugging off his saddlebags.

'I'll just put some of my special ointment on my paws before I go, if you don't mind,' he said. 'A dog in my business has to look after his pads.'

Quickly he flipped one of the bags open.

All sorts of things spilled out onto the grass. Shiny, glittery things, brightly coloured scarves, interesting little packets and boxes …

Everyone craned forward to look. Raymond pawed casually through the things and shook his head.

'Silly me, it must be in the other one,' he murmured.

He opened the other bag, and soon there was another pile of fascinating objects beside the first. Everything was very wonderful, but Scruffy was relieved to see nothing that looked like a sausage, rubber or otherwise.

Raymond selected a small bubble of plastic and pierced it carefully with a blunt claw. Pink creamy stuff oozed out of the bubble, and he began to rub it into the pads of his back paws.

'Ah!' he sighed. 'That feels better. Wonderful stuff, this. I haven't had a cracked pad since I started using it.'

'How much are the scarves?' asked Mavis, eyeing a bright blue one enviously.

'Oh, those?' Raymond looked up absent-mindedly. 'Seven dog treats a piece.'

Mavis looked disappointed. She didn't have even *one* dog treat. She wasn't very fond of them. As she often said, she preferred a nice fat thistle any day.

Raymond seemed suddenly to notice her expression.

'Oh, did you *want* a scarf?' he exclaimed. 'Oh, well, if that's the case I could make a special deal for you. Since you've all been so kind. For you – five dog treats. Can't do any better than that, I'm afraid, much as I'd like to. These particular scarves are very high quality. They cost me six.'

Mavis shook her head and turned away. 'Thanks very much,' she muttered. 'But –'

'Oh, I'm so sorry!' Raymond looked distressed. 'I shouldn't have mentioned it. I didn't realise things here were a little bit – tight, shall we say? I thought that in this magnificent house, the house of heroes, finding a mere five dog treats would be easy. My mistake.'

'Not at all!' exclaimed Barney, very unwilling to lose the admiration of this intelligent stranger.

He turned to Mavis.

'I'll buy the scarf for you, Mavis,' he said grandly. 'Why not? Plenty of dog treats inside.'

'Oh, thank you, Barney,' said Mavis in surprise.

'Now, what a generous gesture,' said Raymond with admiration. He watched under his eyebrows as Barney lumbered into the house.

'Sucked in,' jeered Max 2 under his breath. But even as he spoke he was looking longingly at a bright yellow ball that lay gleaming among the other goods that had rolled out of one of the saddlebags.

He nudged his twin.

'How much is the yellow ball?' Max 1 asked, as if he didn't really care at all.

'Now, haven't you got an eye for a bargain, young dog?' said Raymond admiringly.

He took the yellow ball and balanced it on the end of his nose.

'This is the very last ball I have, so it's going cheap,' he said. 'Four dog biscuits only.'

The Maxes glanced at one another. 'Two dog biscuits,' said Max 1 boldly. 'And not a biscuit more.'

Raymond looked shocked and regretful, and took the ball from his nose.

'Sorry,' he said. 'I'd like to oblige you – I really would. But those balls are very special items. They've been snapped up everywhere I've been. A Scotch Terrier not far from here took the second-last one, only half an hour ago.'

'Tiger?' exclaimed Max 2. '*Tiger's* got one of those balls?'

Raymond nodded cheerfully.

'I believe that was the name,' he said. 'A clever little chap with heavy whiskers. Wearing a fine quality red-checked coat. Friend of yours, is he?'

The Maxes nodded. Now that they knew Tiger had one of the yellow balls, they were both crazy to have one too. But four dog biscuits! That was very expensive. They hesitated.

'Tell you what,' said Raymond, leaning forward and lowering his voice. 'I like you. I really do. So I'll give you the ball for three biscuits. As long as you promise not to tell anyone else.'

The Maxes nodded gleefully.

'Don't go away!' said Max 1. 'We'll be right back!'

He and Max 2 turned and scurried back to their own house. They knew they could reach the dog biscuit box by standing on each other's shoulders. They'd done it many times before, in an emergency.

Barney returned with the five dog treats. Some were rather fluffy, because they'd been hidden under his blanket, but Raymond didn't seem to mind. He counted them carefully and tucked them away in one of his bags. Then he gave Mavis the blue scarf.

Mavis looked at it lovingly. It was so wonderful that she couldn't decide whether to wear it or eat it. At last she twined it around her horns, where she was sure it would look very attractive, as well as discouraging the birds from roosting on her head.

'Magnificent!' said Raymond. 'And to think that unpleasant dog from behind The Long High Wall told me that there was no point in coming down here.'

'Garbage Guts?' snarled Barney in a fury. 'Did *he* buy something from you?'

Raymond nodded. 'Sadly, we poor salesdogs must do business with all sorts,' he said. 'We can't pick and choose. The dog of whom you speak – well, it's probably better not to go into details, but, of course, he was not what I would call a gentledog.'

'What did he buy?' asked Max 1, eaten up with curiosity.

Raymond shrugged. 'My finest rope ladder,' he said. 'One of the scarves – a red one – for disguise, I believe. And some false claws.' He shook his head. 'I fear he was up to no good. But what could I do? He had biscuits and treats to spend, and a poor dog must live.'

'Of course you must,' said Gina generously. 'Obviously, you have a hard life.'

Raymond turned to her with a charming smile.

'Perhaps. But being able to meet and serve dogs as beautiful as you, dear lady, makes it all worthwhile. Do you know what I would choose for you, if it was up to me?'

He picked up a beautiful silver neck chain and let

it slip through his paws, so that the sunlight glinted on the shining links.

'Oh, I couldn't possibly afford that,' cried Gina, in a flutter.

'Just for the pleasure of seeing you wear this, I'd cut the price to the bone,' said Raymond, displaying the glittering chain temptingly. 'Six biscuits and four treats. Practically a gift.'

Gina hesitated.

'Should I?' she whispered to Scruffy. 'I could just manage it. I checked the dog biscuits only this morning, and I'm sure I've got six left. But it's so *expensive!*'

Scruffy didn't know what to say. The chain was pretty, there was no doubt about that. It would suit Gina very well. And it was practically a gift, Raymond had said. But still …

The silver chain flashed in the sun.

'Go on, Gina,' said Mavis, turning her head this way and that to admire the shape of her shadow on the grass.

In the trees, the birds were chattering indignantly. Mavis tossed her scarf-draped horns at them in triumph.

'I'll do it!' Gina exclaimed. She ran off, heading for home.

17 May Your Troubles Be Little Ones

Scruffy followed Gina. She wanted to get something from home as well.

Her treats and biscuits were in a cupboard that was far too high for her to reach, but her special-occasion bone, her most precious possession, was somewhere in the garden. If only she could think where she had buried it! Surely it would be enough to buy something.

She concentrated until she thought her brain was going to explode, and finally she remembered. The special-occasion bone was buried under an overhanging bush, beside the fish pond. She had thought it would be handy to have water nearby, for drinks between chews, the next time she dug it up.

She rushed to the spot, and began digging in a frenzy of excitement. But when at last she found the bone, she was disappointed. It was quite a bit smaller than she remembered – just a shadow of its former self.

Scruffy realised that she must have eaten more of it than she thought, the last time there was a special occasion. And her second-best bone, she knew, was even smaller.

Gina was already on her way back to Barney's house. There was nothing more to be done. Scruffy picked up the remains of the special-occasion bone, and trailed after her friend.

The sun had gone behind some clouds, which were growing darker and heavier by the moment. It seemed to Scruffy that the clouds matched her mood.

She felt quite depressed. She would have loved to

buy something special from Raymond. Now she doubted that she would be able to afford anything at all.

By the time Gina and Scruffy reached Barney's front garden, Raymond had already taken the Maxes' payment, and, balancing the yellow ball teasingly on his nose, was beginning to pack up his bags.

'I don't like the look of those clouds,' he said, passing the chain to Gina and taking her biscuits and treats with a bow. 'I'd better be on my way.'

'Frightened of a little bit of rain, are you?' Barney joked, nudging him in the ribs.

'I walk in all weathers, rain or shine, my friend,' said Raymond cheerfully, bouncing the yellow ball on his nose in the cleverest way. 'But you dogs are used to finer living, and I wouldn't keep you outside in the wet for the world.'

'Before you go, could I buy something with this?' Scruffy asked timidly, putting her special-occasion bone on the grass. Even to her eyes it looked pitifully small, and of course it was covered in dirt.

Raymond raised his shaggy eyebrows and the Maxes snorted with laughter behind their paws. Scruffy felt crushed.

'I really don't have anything … Oh, wait!' said Raymond.

Still balancing the yellow ball on his nose, he dug into the bottom of one of the bags, and brought out a small, round, yellow-brown object, strangely wrinkled.

'This is perfect for you, my friend, since digging is your particular talent,' he said solemnly. 'If carefully buried, it will turn into something amazing, I'm told. What do you say?'

Scruffy eyed the yellow-brown object doubtfully. It looked vaguely familiar. Really, it wasn't the sort of purchase she'd had in mind.

As she hesitated, Raymond looked up. The first drops of rain were falling. He closed his saddlebags, and slung them over his back once more.

'Tell you what,' he said to Scruffy, pushing the yellow-brown thing into her paws. 'You just keep this. No charge. It's the least I can do.'

'Thank you very much,' said Scruffy, though, to tell the truth, she didn't feel particularly grateful.

'And now, I must be off,' said Raymond.

He turned to the rest of the dogs.

'It's been a great pleasure to meet you,' he said. 'I can't think when I've spent a happier hour. Thank you all!' He laughed, nudging Barney playfully with his shoulder. 'Especially you, Barney. May your troubles be little ones.'

With that, he handed the yellow ball to Max 1 and trotted away, disappearing as he went through the swampy ground, and soon appearing again on the road.

He waved cheerfully and hurried on, past Barney's house and the Maxes' house, and on up the hill.

Ignoring the rain, which had started to fall more heavily now, the Dolan Street dogs waved until he was out of sight.

'A marvellous canine,' said Barney, as they turned away from the gate. '"May your troubles be little ones," indeed. What a lovely old-fashioned farewell.'

'*You've* changed your tune,' said Max 1, grinning as he practised balancing the yellow ball on his nose, as Raymond had done.

Barney scratched himself thoughtfully.

'Not at all,' he said. 'I just know a gentledog when

I see one. When you're as old as I am, young Max, you'll learn –'

The dogs never found out what Max 1 was going to learn, for just at that moment the yellow ball bounced from his nose, landed on a prickly bush, and burst with a small pop.

Everyone jumped and stumbled backwards. Then Max 1 and Max 2 crept forward again and stared in disbelief at the limp scrap of yellow rubber that was all that remained of their beautiful ball.

'You broke it, you bird!' Max 2 yelled to his brother.

'What do you mean, I broke it?' Max 1 shouted back. 'I didn't touch it! It broke itself, on that bush. Balls aren't supposed to do that. Especially balls that cost three dog biscuits!'

Narrowing her eyes against the rain, Mavis moved forward and delicately touched the yellow scrap with the tip of her tongue.

'Yes,' she said, nodding. 'I thought so. It's not a real ball at all. It's just a balloon blown up small. Or was. You really should be more careful about what you buy, you two.'

She saw that everyone was looking at her.

'What?' she demanded.

Barney cleared his throat and scratched uncomfortably.

'Your hair, Mavis,' he murmured. 'It's … well, not to beat around the bush, it's …'

'*Blue!*' chorused Max 1 and Max 2. Their own troubles forgotten, they fell to the ground, helpless with laughter.

Mavis stared at them haughtily. A bright blue drip ran down her nose and dropped onto her left front foot. She stared at it, blinking, as if she couldn't believe her eyes.

'I'm afraid the colour in your scarf is washing out in the rain, Mavis,' said Scruffy, struggling not to laugh herself. 'It must have been just ink, or something.'

The giggles were almost bursting in her throat. The matter was serious, but Mavis certainly did look funny. The more the rain fell, the more the colour of her scarf faded, and the more her horns, head and ears changed to brightest blue.

'This is an outrage!' hissed Mavis.

She tossed the scarf from her head. It fell to the grass beside the burst balloon – a limp, greyish piece of cloth, looking more and more like an old stained white handkerchief every moment.

'Raymond conned us!' gasped Max 2. 'He –'

He broke off to stare at Gina's chain. The silver colour was peeling off in the rain and dropping in little curled flakes onto Gina's fur, leaving what seemed to be a flimsy white plastic chain behind.

Scruffy couldn't bear to look. Six dog biscuits and four treats, for a painted plastic chain! It was too awful.

Gina pulled at her chain. It came apart in her paws. She threw it on the ground beside the handkerchief and the burst balloon.

'So that's that,' she said sadly. 'I might have known.'

'No wonder Raymond wanted to get away quickly!'

exclaimed Max 1. 'He knew our ball would burst as soon as we started playing with it, and that everything else would fall apart in the rain.'

'Scruffy's thing hasn't fallen apart,' said Gina, looking at the wizened object in Scruffy's paw. 'And she got it free.'

'Raymond only gave it to me because he wanted to get rid of it,' said Scruffy. 'So I don't think it counts.'

She sniffed cautiously at the yellow-brown thing, and suddenly realised what it was. An idea began to stir in her mind.

'I wonder if Tiger's balloon has burst yet,' said Max 2. He and Max 1 started roaring with laughter again.

After a moment, Gina and Mavis started laughing too.

'This is no laughing matter!' thundered Barney, shaking his ears violently and biting at his front paws one after the other. 'That dog is a criminal! He should be locked up! I didn't like his looks from the start! Didn't I tell you?'

No one said anything. Barney was upset enough. Even the Maxes couldn't see the point of making him angrier.

'"May your troubles be little ones," he says,' growled Barney bitterly, gnawing at his elbow.

'Giggling away! He knew all the time. The swine!'

Bewildered, Gina moved closer to Barney, wanting to comfort him.

'Keep away from me!' shouted Barney. 'Don't touch me!'

Gina stopped dead, surprised and hurt.

'I don't know why you're so crabby, Barney,' said Max 1. 'You didn't get anything from Raymond. Anything personal.'

'I did,' said Barney grimly. 'As it happens, I got something *very* personal from him.'

The other dogs stared.

'*Very* personal,' Barney muttered, scratching violently. 'And if you must know, I'll tell you. My troubles *are* little ones. *That rotten, shaggy mongrel gave me fleas!*'

There was a terrible silence. Then Mavis's lips twitched.

'At least he didn't charge you for them,' she said.

Everyone laughed, and finally even Barney started to smile.

'Get on home, you dogs,' he said, his grin growing broader even as he scratched. 'Friends share their troubles, but I don't want you to share these. My bones, they itch!'

18 Rich Dog, Poor Dog

Next morning, the sun was out, the sky was clear, and Barney was feeling himself again. Or, as Max 1 said, he was at least not feeling the fleas.

'I always make it a rule to keep some flea soap on hand,' Barney said, when the dogs arrived in his yard. 'Just as well, too. We've got visitors tonight. Pets *and* Petlings.'

'Well, if they caught fleas from you, you'd just have to lend them your flea soap, wouldn't you, Barney?' said Mavis sensibly.

Barney looked doubtful. 'There isn't much left,' he said.

'I take pills for fleas,' said Gina. 'Like the ones they advertise on "Dog Hospital".'

'So do we,' said Max 2.

'*You* don't,' said his brother. 'You always spit yours out.'

'Only when Sal doesn't put enough honey on it,' Max 2 protested.

'Garbage!' snorted Barney. 'How could a pill hurt a flea?'

Gina tried to explain it to him, but he wouldn't listen. He said flea soap had been good enough for Old Buster, and it was good enough for him.

Scruffy didn't join the argument. She had never thought about fleas before, and wasn't sure what she did about them. Perhaps, she thought, goats didn't get fleas.

Anyway, she had other things on her mind. One

was a worrying thing. The other was exciting. The two together made her feel all churned up inside.

'How do you like my hair, by the way?' Mavis asked.

She had left her head out in the rain for an hour the previous day. Now it was no longer bright blue, but a rather attractive silver-grey colour.

'It's lovely,' said Gina.

'It really suits you,' Scruffy added.

Mavis nodded, and tossed her horns.

'It won't last,' she said carelessly. 'But it's nice for a change.'

She was still eating breakfast. It was the remains of her scarf, and she seemed to be enjoying it.

'I missed the early news,' Scruffy burst out. 'What did it say?'

She had been hoping she wouldn't have to ask, but no one had said anything, and she couldn't wait any longer.

She had to know what the birds had said about the terrible results of Raymond's visit. She had to know if stories were spreading about Dolan Street all over again.

'I was scared to listen to the news, I'm afraid,' murmured Gina.

'We weren't scared. But we didn't hear it,' said Max 2.

'We never do,' yawned his brother. 'The early news is too early.'

'Oh, Barney and I heard it,' said Mavis, carefully turning the scarf around to start on a fresh corner. 'There was an item about my hair, of course.'

'W – was there?' Scruffy stammered. Her stomach seemed to be tying itself into knots.

Barney smiled broadly, and stretched.

'Indeed,' he said. 'Fortunately, because of the rain, the birds only saw Mavis's hair late in the day, when it wasn't so – ah – *bright* as it was at first. The item was very flattering.'

He puffed out his chest. 'I think, in fact, Mavis has started a trend,' he added.

'And there was nothing else about Dolan Street?' Gina asked eagerly. 'Nothing about my necklace, or the yellow ball, or ... um ... fleas?'

'No,' said Barney triumphantly. 'I told you. The birds were hiding from the rain, weren't they? They didn't see a thing.'

'So it was just like the day we saved the world,' said Max 1. 'No one will ever know anything about it.'

'That's right,' Barney said. He looked very contented. Even more so than Scruffy would have expected.

'Was there anything else?' she asked timidly.

'A few little things,' said Barney. He licked a paw thoughtfully, while everyone waited in suspense. Finally, he looked up.

'If you dogs got up early enough you'd know for yourselves,' he said. 'Always remember, as Old Buster, rest his bones, used to say: The early dog gets the biggest biscuit. But all right, I'll tell you. The second news will be on any minute, anyway. It seems our friend Garbage Guts had an unfortunate accident yesterday.'

'What?' Everyone leaned forward.

'Yes,' said Barney. 'It seems he was climbing a rope ladder, trying to escape over The Long High Wall. The ladder was faulty. Rope was rotten, or something. And because he was wearing *very* shoddy false claws, which fell to pieces as soon as he grabbed really hard with them, he didn't have a chance of saving himself. ' He shook his head. 'As the reporter said, for a great escaper he acted very foolishly. Buying a rotten ladder. And the claws were another mistake.'

'Is he badly injured?' quavered Gina.

'Dead?' asked Max 1 hopefully.

'He was lucky,' said Barney. His lips twitched with pleasure. 'He has a very badly bruised – ah – behind. Having fallen, tail first, onto a small pile of bricks.'

Scruffy winced, imagining it.

'Apparently he looked a real bird when he was found,' added Mavis, swallowing the last of her scarf. 'The rain had started by then. He was all twisted up in old rope, and he was *howling*. He had a pale pink mask over his nose, and all this red stuff was dripping onto the road. He thought he was bleeding to death.'

'Oh, no!' Gina covered her face with her paws.

The Maxes fell to the ground, laughing.

'So he won't be doing much escaping for a while,' Barney said, with great satisfaction. 'Or boasting, either, I'd say.'

Just then, the second morning news began. The story about Mavis of Dolan Street's attractive new hair colour was repeated. It was a rather gushing report, Scruffy thought, but Mavis was pleased.

After that, there was a much longer item about how a rascally so-called travelling salesdog called Raymond had fooled dozens of neighbourhood dogs by selling them shoddy goods at very high prices.

The biggest bird of all, the reporter said, had turned out to be Garbage Guts, from behind The Long High Wall.

'The self-proclaimed "great escaper" is sporting a heavily bandaged tail this morning,' the reporter finished nastily, after giving a report of the collapse of the rope ladder. 'He won't be sitting down for quite a while, they say.'

Several eyewitnesses added their stories. Garbage Guts had fallen to the ground *outside* the wall, it seemed, so dozens of dogs had seen the accident, and heard his howls.

'There *are* disadvantages, you see, in living shoulder to shoulder with a lot of other dogs,' said Barney. 'No way you can hush anything up, when you live on a busy road.'

Everyone nodded agreement. Even the Maxes.

Scruffy thought it was time to tell her news. A little nervously, she pushed forward the round yellow-brown thing that Raymond had given her.

'I've worked out what this is,' she said. 'It's an old, rotten apple.'

'Even Garbage Guts wouldn't eat a rotten apple,' Max 2 snorted, wrinkling his nose in disgust.

'I'm not going to eat it,' said Scruffy. 'But I was thinking … apples have seeds inside them. If I plant this, an apple tree might grow.'

'*Apple* tree?' said Mavis, very interested.

'Yes. And I thought it might be just the thing for your field, Mavis,' said Scruffy, rather shyly. 'I've seen apple trees on TV. They're not too big, and not too small. They lose their leaves in winter. They have nice-smelling flowers in spring, and apples grow on the branches later on. We could watch it grow together.'

'*Apples*?' Mavis looked *very* pleased. 'Well, if I'd known apples grew on trees, I would have asked for an apple tree long ago. That will be perfect!'

'As long as you remember not to eat it, Mavis,' said Gina anxiously. 'When it starts to grow, I mean.'

'I wouldn't eat it!' Mavis said, shocked. 'I wouldn't eat our own tree!' She paused. 'But – the apples that grow on it …?' she enquired delicately.

'Oh, you can eat the apples!' said Scruffy. 'Whenever you like.' She glanced at the others. 'I might even have one or two myself,' she added boldly, but no one said anything.

They decided that there was just time to do the planting before 'Dog Hospital' started. So, with Scruffy proudly in the lead, they trooped down to the field behind the house.

While Mavis tried to decide exactly where the tree should be planted, Scruffy leaned against the wire

fence, the wrinkled apple held carefully between her paws.

The hens were strolling around the Maxes' back yard. They had got out of the hen house again and were enjoying their freedom, busily pecking at the grass and chatting to one another.

It was boring sort of talk, Scruffy thought. Just, 'Will you look at the stripes on this grub!' and 'Wasn't that a nice bit of bacon rind this morning?' and 'My wing's itchy' – that sort of thing. Nothing anyone would find interesting.

She was glad that she wasn't going to have them for neighbours. Even when the apple tree grew, the field wouldn't be nearly as nice as home.

A hen looked through the wire. It was Daisy. Her little black eyes sparkled as she noticed the apple.

'I'll take that old thing off your paws if you like, dog,' she crooned. 'I'm not fussy.'

'Sorry,' said Scruffy, moving the apple further away. 'We need it. Where's Peck today?'

'Peck?' cackled Daisy. 'Oh, don't talk to me about *Peck*. She's gone broody. All she does is sit on her eggs all day. All she can talk about is chickens. And knitting. She's no fun any more. Well, see you! Tell Mavis I like her hair.'

And she stalked off.

🦴🦴🦴

Mavis changed her mind several times about exactly where the apple tree should go, but at last she settled on a spot.

Scruffy dug a hole. Then, with all her friends standing around her, she carefully planted the apple, and filled the hole in again.

'I'm sure it will grow,' said Mavis confidently.

'And that, at least, will be *something* we got from Raymond,' said Barney. 'He mightn't have appreciated it. But *we* will.'

Everyone cheered.

Scruffy looked around at her friends and suddenly thought of Raymond, trudging along alone, his saddlebags heavy with biscuits and dog treats.

No doubt he was laughing to himself as he thought how rich he was, and what fools the Dolan Street dogs had been.

But now we know what he's like, and so does everyone else in the neighbourhood, so he'll never risk coming back here, Scruffy thought. And it will be the same everywhere he goes. Because everywhere he visits, he makes enemies instead of friends.

'No wonder Raymond thought the old apple was worthless,' she said aloud. 'Raymond could never stay in one place long enough to watch a tree grow. He wouldn't dare.'

'That's right,' Gina said. 'Poor Raymond.'

'*Poor Raymond*?' roared Max 1, Max 2 and Barney.

But Scruffy knew that Gina was right.

Raymond will never have a home like Dolan Street, she thought. He'll never have friends like we have. So who's rich and who's poor, in the end?

And as she turned to face the others – Max 1 and Max 2 shouting, Gina smiling, Barney grumbling and Mavis happily chewing a thistle – Scruffy was very sure of the answer to that.

∽∽∽

The next day, as soon as the Pets had left in their cars, the dogs joined Barney on his front grass and listened to the news. It was just as interesting as it had been the day before.

A gang of burglars, a *real* gang of burglars this time, had raided the house on Danger Corner.

The burglars had offered the Rottweilers bribes of meat, apparently, and the Rottweilers had accepted. Then, since the Danger Corner Pets were out, the burglars had simply walked into the house and cleaned it out. Not a stick of furniture remained in the place, the news said.

'Imagine accepting a bribe!' gasped Gina, very shocked.

'Why not?' said Max 2. 'You could always go back on your word afterwards. Get the food down quick, then stop the robbers anyway.'

'No you couldn't!' Scruffy exclaimed.

'Of course you could,' said Max 1, yawning. 'Don't you know anything? Promises to burglars don't count.'

Scruffy lay back on the grass again. It was too pleasant to argue. The sun was warm. The grass was smooth. The sky was brightest blue.

Gina glanced up at the birds twittering respectfully in the trees above them.

'They're behaving very well these days, aren't they?' she murmured.

'It won't last,' Max 2 grunted. 'Birds are birds. They can't help themselves.'

'That's right,' Barney agreed. 'As Old Buster told me, time and again –'

He broke off abruptly.

At first Scruffy thought it was because the Maxes had groaned and put their paws over their ears, but she soon realised it wasn't.

Barney was listening to something. A little deaf he might be, but there was one sound he never failed to hear.

A truck was coming down the Dolan Street hill.

Barney waited, motionless. The truck reached his fence, slid past it, squeaked to a stop, then slowly turned.

No one said a word.

The truck began moving back up the hill again.

Barney got to his feet. He shook himself, once, twice, three times. Then he walked slowly to the side of the house.

The dogs waited. From the side of Barney's house there was no sound. The minutes crawled by.

'He's done it!' whispered Gina, her eyes bright with excitement. 'He must have done it at last! He's been away much longer than usual. Oh, this is so *strange*! Oh, it makes me shiver all over!'

She shivered, to prove it.

At that moment, Barney came slowly back around the house and padded towards them. He was smiling slightly, and licking his lips.

Scruffy's heart thudded. She glanced at Max 1 and Max 2. They were looking very alert, and for once they had nothing to say.

'Well? Well?' Gina shrieked, jumping to her feet. 'Barney! Did it work? Did it?'

Barney reached them, and sat down.

'Put it this way,' he said, and licked his lips again. 'I'm making progress.'

'There was a sausage in your bowl?' gasped Scruffy.

'Not quite. But there was … *half a sausage roll*.'

The dogs stared.

'You see?' said Barney. 'I've nearly got it right. All I

have to do is keep trying for the full sausage, without the pastry. As I've always said, if at first you don't succeed –'

'You had visitors for dinner last night, Barney,' Max 1 interrupted, quite rudely.

'So?' said Barney.

'There were Petlings here,' said Max 2. 'We heard them yapping. Petlings like sausage rolls. *I* think –'

'*Some* dogs,' said Barney, raising his voice, 'have an answer for everything. And *some* dogs will never accept what is plain for everyone else to see. It is their loss, in my opinion.'

'Hear! Hear!' said Mavis.

Max 1 and Max 2 muttered to one another behind their paws. Scruffy thought she heard the words 'old fleabag', but she wasn't sure.

Barney lay down. 'Ah, well. Half a sausage roll is better than none, I always say,' he murmured.

And, smiling, he licked the last drop of sauce from his whiskers.

THE AUTHOR

Emily Rodda is one of Australia's most versatile and gifted writers for children. Her first book, *Something Special*, was published in 1986, and since then five of her novels (*Something Special*, *Pigs Might Fly*, *The Best-kept Secret*, *Finders Keepers* and *Rowan of Rin*) have won the Children's Book Council of Australia's Book of the Year (Younger Readers) Award.

Emily is the author of the popular series *Deltora Quest*, *The Three Doors* and *Rondo* trilogies and the *Rowan* novels.

In 1995 she was awarded the Dromkeen Medal for her outstanding contribution to Australian children's literature.

Also by Emily Rodda from Omnibus Books

Rowan of Rin

To the villagers of Rin the boy Rowan is a timid weakling. Yet it is his help they need when the stream that flows from the top of the Mountain dries up. Without its water their precious bukshah herds will die, and Rin will be doomed.

The six strongest villagers must brave the unknown terrors of the Mountain to discover the answer to the riddle. And Rowan, the unwanted seventh member of the group, must go with them.

This exciting fantasy adventure is the first book in the popular *Rowan* series.

Children's Book Council of Australia
Book of the Year (Younger Readers), 1994

The five books in the series are:
Rowan of Rin
Rowan and the Travellers
Rowan and the Keeper of the Crystal
Rowan and the Zebak
Rowan of the Bukshah

Also by Emily Rodda from Omnibus Books

The Rondo Trilogy

The old music box, with its strict rules, has been handed down through Leo's family. When the rules are broken, Leo's life is changed forever as he and his cousin Mimi plunge into a thrilling quest in the fantastic world of Rondo.

The Key to Rondo was shortlisted for CBCA Book of the Year (Younger Readers) in the 2008 Awards; the Patricia Wrightson Prize in the 2008 New South Wales Premier's Literary Awards; and the 2008 Australian Book Industry Awards. It was also a finalist in Best Children's (8–12 years) Long Fiction in the 2007 Aurealis Awards and won the Older Readers category of the 2008 KOALA Awards. *The Wizard of Rondo* was winner, Best Children's (8–12 years) Long Fiction in the 2008 Aurealis Awards and shortlisted in the CBCA Book of the Year Awards in 2009.

The Key to Rondo
The Wizard of Rondo
The Battle for Rondo

The Three Doors Trilogy

Three magic Doors you here behold
Time to choose: Wood? Silver? Gold?
Listen to your inner voice
And you will make the wisest choice.

Rye is willing to risk everything to save his brothers, lost in the terrifying land outside the towering Wall of Weld. Sonia is determined to find and destroy the Enemy who is sending the ferocious flying beasts called skimmers to ravage the city.

The companions battle the perils behind the gold and silver Doors. But Weld is still under threat, and Rye knows what he has to do. One Door remains a mystery – the ancient wooden Door that he has been drawn to from the beginning. For good or ill, his desperate quest will end beyond that Door.

All he has to do is dare to go through it.

The Golden Door
The Silver Door
The Third Door

Deltora Quest

Deltora lies in decay, held in the Shadow Lord's cruel grip. Its towns are in ruins, its desperate people struggle to survive, and strange, cruel beasts prowl the land and slide through its putrid waterways.

Three determined companions seek the seven gems that must be restored to the ancient Belt of Deltora – for without its magic the evil Shadow Lord can never be overthrown.

There are fifteen books in the three series of Deltora Quest:

1

The Forests of Silence
The Lake of Tears
The City of the Rats
The Shifting Sands
Dread Mountain
The Maze of the Beast
The Valley of the Lost
Return to Del